babylove

I. S. Belle

KDP ISBN: 979-8-398-98962-5

IngramSpark ISBN: 978-0-473-66832-7

content warnings

Hi guys! A brief content warning before we get started.

Content warnings: harm to children, animal death, gore, bullying, drug use, smoking, swearing.

Shaking with anguish, fear, and pain,
She kissed and kissed her with a hungry mouth.
—— Christina Rossetti, Goblin Market

chapter
one

EVEN WITH THE BLOOD, rituals and resurrections, the most surprising thing about the summer of 2003 was Ivy Wexler.

Frankie Tanner was in her usual lunchtime haze when Ivy marched up. It took a second to realize Ivy was, in fact, looking at her, and not just leaning her hip against Frankie's table for a place to rest.

Frankie blinked up at her through clumpy mascara. The pleasant blur from smoking up in the bathrooms faded into the background, the real world coming into sharp, irritating focus. Meatloaf stench from the tray in front of her. Low hum of Bulldeen High, all whispers and unkind laughs.

Ivy motioned for Frankie to remove her headphones.

With a scowl, Frankie did. "What do you want, princess?"

Ivy gave a short and surprised chuckle. They'd talked before—in a small town like Bulldeen, it was impossible for them not to—but this was the first time they'd spoken directly since first grade, when Ivy found her crying behind the swings. Frankie had a faint, improbable memory of Ivy's arm around her shoulders, her soft voice in Frankie's ear. *Everything's going to be alright.* Sometimes Frankie thought it was a dream. It was difficult to reconcile that gentle version with the girl who stood in front of her now, shiny and intimidating, the first freshman they let onto the cheerleading team in decades.

Ivy beamed, flicking her straightened hair away from her heart-shaped face. "Your sister says you're going to have to do summer school if you don't pass a make-up test for Mr. Clack."

Frankie looked across the cafeteria to where April Tanner sat. April tipped her head back to laugh at what Frankie assumed was a bad joke, since that was definitely her sister's fake laugh.

April wasn't looking their way. She never looked at her little sister while they were at school. Why would she? They were in entirely different social circles. As in, April Tanner *had* a social circle. She hung with the other cheerleaders and, on occasion, Bulldeen Bulls footballers.

Frankie was a one-woman band. She preferred it that way, and if anyone tried poking holes in this theory, she just said it louder.

"Well?" Ivy cocked her head expectantly. More pale hair fell into her face. "Are you failing or aren't you?"

Frankie reached for her headphones. "Go mess with somebody else, Ivy. I promise I'm very unsatisfying to taunt."

"I'm not *taunting* you. God." Ivy rolled her eyes. "I'm asking if you want help."

"Help," Frankie repeated, unable to stop the incredulous smile. "*You* want to help *me*."

"For a favor, of course."

"Oh! Here I thought you were doing this out of the goodness of your heart."

Ivy's next laugh cut off abruptly. She rubbed the corner of her mouth, slim fingers twitching as if resisting the urge to cover it. *That would be a shame*, Frankie thought, and then squashed that thought into a manageable size to store away and never look at again.

Frankie rested her chin on her hands, rings digging into her jaw. "So what is it? Drug deal? Oooh, do you need me to kneecap someone? I don't hurt kids. Well, maybe for the right price."

"Good to know," Ivy said, bright and only a little mocking. "Look. I'm a good tutor. Do you want to help, or do you want to be stuck listening to Mr. Clack talk about Moby Dick for the rest of the summer?"

"You still haven't told me what it is I'm helping with, princess."

Ivy's mouth pulled under her twitching fingers. She was still rubbing, red gloss glinting at the corner of her pinkie where she'd swiped her lips by accident.

"I need—"

An arm looped around Ivy's shoulder, cutting her off. Marvin Martin, mediocre footballer and perpetual polo shirt wearer, grinned at his girlfriend's shocked gasp.

"Whoa, hey! Something got your tongue?" He pinched her chin.

Ivy smiled, so wide and so fake Frankie didn't bother hiding her scoff.

But the smile didn't even falter. "Just fulfilling my end of a bargain. Is there a seat over there for me?"

He frowned. "Yeah, babe, always."

Yeah babe, Frankie mouthed mockingly, rotating her fork in her meatloaf. *Always!*

Ivy twisted to look behind him at the cheerleader table. "Mine looks a little cold. Mind warming it for me?"

She lay a hand on his skinny chest. His confused expression softened.

"Alright," he said, obviously not fooled, but not prying. He lingered by the table long enough that Frankie shot him a dangerous look. Why didn't the black lipstick, piercings and knife tricks in the parking lot make people leave her the hell alone? It made them ignore her, sure. But it didn't protect her from this shit.

Marvin's annoying grin slid back into place. "Hey, Loser Tanner. Coming to the party next weekend?"

"You know me," Frankie deadpanned. "I am the party queen."

"I bet." Marvin's squinty dishwater eyes got even squintier. "You totally should. It'll be fun."

"Marvin," Ivy said. "My chair."

"Right, yeah." He didn't look at her. "Come on, don't be like that. We're inviting everybody. We're inviting, uh—" He looked around for more undesirables, gaze landing on the dead freaks—so named due to a certain bully always leaving them with a menacing *you're dead, freaks*—clustered around their usual table.

Marvin cupped his hands around the yell. "HEY DEAD FREAKS! WANNA COME TO MY GIRLFRIEND'S PARTY NEXT WEEKEND? HER PARENTS ARE OUT OF TOWN!"

The dead freaks jumped. There were four of them, all seniors on track to graduate next month: big, outgoing (and in Frankie's opinion, weirdly fashionable) city kid Jules Havelock the only one Frankie found interesting. Then they had haughty, smart Anna Higgins who could have been interesting if only she was haughtier; polite, quiet "Babe" Simmons who was probably a *little* interesting behind closed doors; and, of course aloof, burly "Dude" Marsh, who might be interesting if he was faking all that aloofness, but somehow Frankie bet he wasn't.

Anna's smile was tight as she replied, "Thanks, Marvin.

We'll see how the night goes."

"Everybody's coming," Marvin repeated. "Shit, even loser Tanner is coming! Right, Tanner?"

Frankie weighed up her options. Option one: say nothing. Chance being seen as pathetic instead of distant and cool. Option two: come up with something snarky, which was harder with the weed fuzzing everything up. Chance sounding pathetic. Option three: walk away. Chance looking cowardly. No matter what Frankie did, she was still Loser Tanner: stark opposite of her older, cooler, athletic bitch of a sister, who in that moment was examining a nonexistent chip in her nail.

Frankie decided to sneak dye into April's shampoo later. She opened her mouth to go with a snarky comment—always the most dramatic option—but Ivy talked over her.

"Marvin. My chair."

Marvin waited for Ivy to relent. When her smile only got bigger and shinier, he sighed.

"Yeah, yeah. Going to warm up your chair." He rapped his knuckles on the side of Frankie's tray, making it rattle. "Come hang, weirdo. It'll be fun."

He grinned again, broadcasting to the cafeteria how outside of the joke she was, and Frankie resisted the urge to slam her lunch tray into the side of his head. She wasn't an idiot. She knew when she was being made fun of.

Ivy waited until he was out of earshot before taking a scrap of paper from her pocket. "Come over to mine after school, alright? I'll make it worth your while."

"I know where you live, you're like three streets away from me." Frankie leaned back in her chair, away from the paper Ivy had placed on the table. She meant it as a teasing tactic, something to make Ivy actually explain what was going on, but all she got was the swish of Ivy's cheerleading skirt as she turned towards her gang. Ivy was, much like Frankie's sister, one of those desperate girls who wore her outfit outside of practice. Like it mattered she was cheerleader on a small-town team that only people who would grow old and die here would remember. Okay, so a good portion of the high school population.

Frankie raised her voice. "Hey! You haven't told me what we're doing yet!"

Ivy glanced back, blue eyes flashing. "See you later, Frankie."

It was the eyes, pale and haunting. No, it was her name. Classmates called her Loser Tanner. Teachers called her Francesca. Her parents called her *you. You, turn the music down, I had a late shift last night.* When April deigned to talk to her, she called her sis.

No one called her Frankie. It stunned her into silence long enough for Ivy to sit down in the chair Marvin pulled out and bowed over, provoking another fake laugh Frankie didn't have the energy to scoff at.

Frankie uncurled the paper, still expecting a joke she wasn't in on.

But there was the address, sitting pretty in Ivy's loopy handwriting. *For Frankie*, it said at the bottom.

Frankie touched the *i*. Instead of a dot, there sat a small inky heart.

chapter
two

FRANKIE WAS USED to having the house to herself after school. After work her parents would drink at different bars until late, and April stayed out with friends after her countless extracurriculars. So Frankie was surprised to hear the front door slam shut at four forty-five. She put down a slice of bread and flipped the butter knife in an easy circle. That knife trick was the only useful thing her cousins ever taught her, and she had a habit of fiddling with whatever was in her hands when she got nervous. Hence the rings: the assortment of skulls and crosses weren't just accessories, they were worry beads. And a door opening was always cause for worry. You never knew who would come through.

Her hand relaxed on the butter knife as April flounced into the kitchen, hip-checking Frankie on the way to the fridge.

"Hey sis, how goes it?" April peered into their cheese shelf. They were a cheese-crazy family. If they were going to snack—which was often—it was on cheese. Frankie was in the middle of making a cheese sandwich with the cheap brand. They ran out of fancy brands the day after every shopping trip.

"Thought you'd be—" April reeled back. "Ow!"

Frankie stepped away from the fridge door, which she'd just bounced off April's head.

April rubbed her scalp. They had the same light hair, but Frankie's was hidden under a mask of dye.

Frankie groaned at April's expression. "Oh my god, you're *fine*, your huge hair will protect you."

April flipped her off. "What was that for?"

"The usual! I know you have a problem with—" Frankie gestured at herself: dark clothing, dark lipstick, faux dark hair, not to mention the tongue piercing and the regrettable stick-and-poke tattoo blotching her inner elbow. In fact, April had started ignoring her at middle school a few months before Frankie started buying everything exclusively in murky tones, but in Frankie's mind the two were forever linked. Frankie was a heavy leather jacket and April was that starched cheerleading uniform. If not for the Loser Tanner label, most people would forget they were sisters. They had the same sharp face—the Tanner face, all cheekbones and chin—but April softened it with foundation and pink gloss. Frankie, of course, leaned into it; eyeshadow and contour filing her features into something to cut yourself on.

"—but you could at least distract Marvin when he starts being a dick," Frankie spat. "*Oooh, come to my party! We totally won't tie you to the toilet and take photos!*"

"Ugh, that was *one* time." April ducked out of the way before the fridge door slammed closed. She waggled a half-finished block of cheese. "Missed."

Frankie wrinkled her nose as April peeled the cheese—labeled APRIL'S DO NOT TOUCH in menacing red biro—and took a bite.

"Wait, why are you home? Cheer practice isn't over yet."

"Finished early," April said, muffled by her mouthful. "Beth G. hurt her foot and had to get driven to the hospital.

She wasn't faking it this time, there was blood and everything."

Frankie ran for the living room. Wallet, keys—where was her pocketknife? She always had it on her, though she only ever had to use it to peel apples. It made everyone leave her alone in middle school, but high schoolers were tragically un-menaced.

"It's over there," April called from the kitchen doorway.

Frankie turned. April pointed to the floor next to the couch where Frankie's pocketknife lay.

"Don't want to keep her waiting," April said slyly.

Alarm bells dinged faintly at the back of Frankie's head. Her shoulders were stiff as she pocketed the blade. She wore men's pants not just for the bagginess, but for the deep pockets. Didn't need a bag with pockets this deep.

"What does she want me to do, clean her house? Do some voodoo against some girl she doesn't like?"

"She wouldn't tell me." April bit the corner off her cheese, looking untroubled by her little sister's possible hazing. "Just asked if you were into dark shit."

"What?"

"I know, right?" April waved at her. "Wait there."

Frankie stood stock-still in the living room as April rummaged around in the kitchen. The sound of a zip being unzipped. Did she mean something specific by *don't want to keep her waiting*, or was it vague teasing? April made the occasional comment about Frankie being a little too interested in girls—sitting close to the TV as a kid to watch women's sports, doodling a beautiful young teacher in her binder back when she dared to draw in school, staring at girls a second too long when they passed on the street—but she never came out and said the word. Just alluded to it. Even then, it was couched in double and triple meanings—it was entirely possible *don't want to keep her waiting* had nothing to do with all those times

Frankie let her gaze linger on Ivy in the hallways, or with Frankie's inability to stop pressing her thumbnail into the heart in Ivy's note, which April couldn't know about anyway.

"Wake up!"

Frankie startled, hands barely coming up in time to catch the thing April threw at her. It was her pencil case.

"Thought I lost it," Frankie said. This was a lie. She thought someone had *stolen* it, and going off of the barely-there awkwardness in April's shrug, it *had* been stolen, probably by April's friends.

April scraped her teeth down the cheese, leaving gorge lines. "What are big sisters for?" She flopped down on the couch, reaching for the remote and toeing off her shoes as Frankie headed for the door. "Don't do anything I wouldn't do!"

Frankie gave her the finger and checked over her shoulder to find April was doing it back, expression fond in ways she would never allow outside the house.

Frankie had walked past Ivy's house a hundred times. It had never...*loomed* like this before. It stretched up, the tallest house on the block. Weeds—nothing else grew in Bulldeen except thornfruit—choked the drive. The paint was a dull white, not yet peeling, but the door was bright black. Frankie raised a hand to knock and thought, bizarrely, of the inside of someone's mouth.

The door flew open. Frankie shrank back, shocked.

"Sorry," Ivy said. "I saw you from my window."

She stroked her hair into place. It puffed back up. Thanks to the sweat from cheer practice, the straightening had lost its luster and her light hair had returned to the frizzy curls Frankie remembered from grade school.

Ivy bit the inside of her cheek. "Um, what are you listening to?"

Frankie removed her headphones from around her neck, tucking them into her pocket with her cassette player. Ivy looked surprised they could fit, and Frankie resisted the urge to go on a spiel about men's pockets.

"Let's not do this, okay?" Frankie nodded behind her. "Just tell me whatever it is I'm doing, and I'll see if it's worth summer school."

Ivy nodded. Didn't move out of the doorway. "You don't want to study first? I have snacks."

Frankie stared at her. "Princess, you're telling me what the hell you want me to do or I'm walking out right now."

She turned around. Before she could get all the way down the steps, a hand closed around her wrist.

Small fingers, Frankie thought. Calluses at the tips. How did a cheerleader get calluses like that? Suddenly the hand was gone, whipping back to her side like Frankie had burned her.

Ivy made a funny aborted dip, as if she was about to do an ironic curtsey then thought better of it. "Follow me."

The house wasn't particularly nicer than Frankie's. Same lopsided floorboards, same sized rooms. But it was a lot *cleaner* than the Tanner house, every surface swept, everything put away. The curtains were neat. Each wall was adorned with landscape hangings, deserts and oceans and rolling hills. *Interior design,* Frankie thought. That was what the Tanners lacked: they didn't make aesthetic use of their space. Curtains fell where they may. Things got put down and stayed there, including dust. *Especially* dust. There was no Tanner in Bulldeen who enjoyed vacuuming.

Frankie rolled her skull ring as she was led through the house. The skull was her favorite, adorning the index finger of her right hand. She liked to press her thumb into the eyeholes.

Ivy reached a slanted door at the end of the hallway. She reached up, feeling around the frame until she found the key, huge and bronze and rusting.

Frankie asked, "You have locked rooms in your own house?"

Ivy looked at her, hovering on the edge of speech. It was a struggle. The hovering stretched on long enough that Frankie said, "Oookay. Lead on, Macduff."

The key screeched in the lock. The door swung open. Stairs led down into a dark basement. For the first time, Frankie felt a twinge of genuine fear.

Halfway down the stairs, Ivy looked up. "Are you coming?"

Frankie forced a laugh. "If you brought me down here to kill me, you really should've made me walk in first. Could've... got me from behind, or something."

"I'm not going to *kill* you." She said it too fast for Frankie's liking. Ivy glanced over her shoulder, down into the gloom. "You *are* into dark stuff, right? Witchy stuff?"

"Witchy stuff," Frankie repeated.

"Like—you were into all those witch books in middle school. And you went to that witch movie, like, eight weeks in a row, what was it called? And you and Milly Hart are the only ones who get out those weird books at the library."

Frankie had to blink a few times before it processed. "Aw, I didn't know you were paying attention!"

"Everybody in town knows that stuff." Ivy said, also too fast. She sucked in her cheek, biting the inside again. She was nervous about *something*.

"Right. New plan: tell me up here."

"It's *really* easier if I show you."

"Yeah, I'm not walking down into that horrifying basement."

"I'll find the light, just give me—"

A yowl split the air. Frankie jumped, almost slipped against the first stair. She grabbed the railing just in time, stumbling forwards. Out of the light of the hallway.

"My cat," Ivy confessed. "Okay? Something is...*wrong* with my cat."

"So? Call the Higginses!"

"It's not something a vet can fix! If you—"

Crack.

Ivy's eyes widened. "Oh shit."

She turned, sprinting into the dark. Glass crashed.

Frankie took a hesitant step forward. "Ivy?"

Fumbling noises, more swearing. The basement lit up, and Ivy appeared at the base of the stairs, waving her down with...a baseball bat?

"Come on!"

Screw it, Frankie decided. If this was a trick, Ivy put a lot of effort into it. She ran down to join Ivy, who was still much more freaked out than Frankie was comfortable with.

"Shit," Ivy chanted. "Shit, shit! I thought the cage would be strong enough!"

"What ca—" Then Frankie saw it: in the corner of the basement, tucked in between a dryer and a washing machine: a small metal cage. Like the rest of the house, it was pristine. Except for the roof, which was busted open. Wires bent backwards where something had forced itself out. Impossible. It was impossible, but—

Bulldeen is a bad place. Unnatural, someone told her once. Who was it?

Ivy ran over to a small, smashed window. Glass littered the grass outside.

"Okay. Okay!" Ivy steepled her fingers in front of her nose. When she turned around, her smile was so manic it jolted a giggle out of Frankie.

"What?" Ivy asked.

Frankie shook her head. "Nothing! Your cat has super strength?"

"I know how it sounds! We just...we have to go find him, he's—"

Another yowl. This one was even more disturbing than the last, an animal in incredible panic and pain. It sounded like a dog. It sounded like nothing Frankie had ever heard.

"Jesus," Frankie said, recoiling. "Whatever's happening, we need to—"

"Right," Ivy said, and raced upstairs.

By the time they followed the noises, the screams were gone. Only low gurgles continued, gurgles and choked whines. Dread clawed its way up Frankie's throat as they approached the end of the backyard.

"It's behind the shed," Ivy whispered. She tightened the grip on her bat.

Frankie slid her pocketknife out. "So what, we're gonna... bash your feral cat's head in?"

"What? No! This is just in case." Ivy angled the bat in front of her, doing a double take when she noticed what Frankie was holding. "Oh, knife, good. Okay, let's go."

Frankie unstuck her feet from the ground. Just a few more steps.

The gurgles stopped. Another noise replaced it: chewing. Slow and satisfied.

No, Frankie thought desperately. Her knife was slippery with sweat. *No no wait I don't want to see...*

But Ivy was still walking, and Frankie was beside her, and the scene revealed itself: first, a fluffy tail. Then the blood. *So* much blood. How didn't they smell it before? The yard stunk of it. Blood coated the yellow grass, the black dirt, the dappled gray fur of the dog it came from. In front of the dog's open stomach crouched a cat. White. Fluffy. Absolutely covered in blood, from its dainty nose to its teeny back paws.

The cat continued to chew, pulling strips off the poor dog's ribs.

"Holy Jesus Christ shit crap god," Frankie heard herself say, nonsensical.

Ivy shushed her, but it was too late. The cat's ear twitched. The chewing stopped.

Frankie grabbed Ivy's arm. "Is it...do we..."

"I don't know," Ivy said. The baseball bat wavered. "I don't—"

The cat turned. Cocked its head.

The girls held their breath.

The cat meowed, a small, unbothered sound, and lifted its paw to wash it. It didn't do much. Its tongue, too, was flushed with red. It was just pushing the blood deeper into its fur.

Frankie let out a shaky breath. Beside her, Ivy did the same, small hands relaxing on her bat.

"I think it was just hungry."

Frankie spluttered. "You—excuse me? It just killed a dog! If this is a joke, you are one messed up girl."

"It's not a joke! I..." Ivy looked towards the fence. Nobody had come running at the dog's screams. Nobody came running in Bulldeen. *Bad place. Unnatural.* Frankie reeled. The resurrection stories were true. The Higginses' grandma coming back. Even Milly Hart, though somehow that felt more dubious—it was easier to believe in a resurrection when the person was gone, a story to be told, rather than someone you saw shuffling around the Shop N' Save.

Ivy's blue eyes were wet. "Is that the Henneseys' dog? They really loved him."

Frankie glanced at the dog's corpse and found she couldn't do it longer than a second without wanting to vomit. "I...yeah, I think so."

"Oh." Ivy's voice trembled. She twisted away, hand worrying at the skin beside her mouth. "Okay," she said to herself. "Okay."

The cat continued grooming. Without the blood it would have been a good-looking cat, all long fur and intelligent eyes.

"What's its name?"

Ivy wiped at her cheeks. "That's Babylove. My granddad's cat. He died last week."

"Oh. I'm sorry."

"No, granddad died last month. *Babylove* died last week." Ivy wiped away fresh tears and turned to face Frankie with dry cheeks.

Frankie stared at her. Stared at the cat, who had actually managed to make some leeway on its front paw, which was pink instead of deep red. Back at Ivy, who stood rigid before her.

"Ivy Wexler. You are *much* more interesting than I gave you credit for."

Ivy's long eyelashes quivered. "You believe me?"

"It's Bulldeen," Frankie said, and the shaky smile she got in return was all the confirmation she needed: she wasn't being made fun of. This was real.

Frankie sucked in a fortifying breath. "Now—what the *hell* did you drag me into?"

three

FRANKIE DID NOT SLEEP that night. She was too busy remembering their hushed conversations in the Wexler bathroom after they put Babylove back in the cage and stacked boxes on the side he'd busted through.

Well, Ivy put him back. Frankie refused to touch him, even though he'd been strangely docile. He'd even given Ivy's callused palm a little lick as she locked the cage. Ivy patted him through the bars, then washed her hands until they were raw.

My granddad gave me a ritual, Ivy told her as she scrubbed. *He said to use it after he passed. But I wanted a trial run, you know? And then Babylove died, and I thought...*

Why waste a good cat corpse, Frankie had said.

Ivy laughed. A good laugh, a true one, not those gaudy ones she threw out at Marvin. Frankie stared at her bedroom ceiling replaying that laugh, the clumsy arch of it, a little too gaspy. Nerves, Frankie figured. The adrenaline of a secret revealed. It had obviously been weighing on Ivy, her shoulders slumping in relief as the words spilled out. The fear of having a feral, superpowered cat hidden in the basement, her parents coming back from visiting family in Toronto in two weeks.

So we have a time limit, Frankie said. Ivy's face had lit up like a Christmas tree, and it wasn't until she was lying in bed that Frankie realized it was because she said *we*.

Frankie slammed her morning alarm quiet before the first beep finished, launching herself out of bed to scribble down the name of a book at her desk. She remembered that this book had made the librarian narrow her eyes that time Frankie had found it on the shelves. The janitor, too, now that Frankie thought about it. That old creep Janitor Larry, always lurking in the stacks, pretending not to judge everything people were reading.

Frankie scribbled some notes under the title: *folk tales— blood giving—nixing spell: how ACCURATE do we need??* She'd been enlisted to make sure the ritual went off perfectly. The ritual Ivy had shown her, scribbled on a crumpled page torn from what looked like a textbook, was more conceptual than practical. Lots of metaphors.

Frankie shuddered, part excitement, part pure dread. *Bulldeen is a bad place. Unnatural.* Who told her? She tried to place the voice, but she couldn't even tell if it was a man or woman.

She went over to her nightstand and slid on her skull ring, twisting it hard around her finger.

"We're not doing anything until we know the nixing spell works."

To control the hunger, Ivy had explained. *I thought I translated it right, but...I guess not.*

Frankie couldn't blame her. The nixing spell was a hasty Latin scribble on the bottom of the ritual, done hastily by the last owner before Granddad Wexler. It was nearly illegible before the coffee stain made it even harder to read. Ivy thought it translated to: *fill the hunger, protect us all.*

Evidently not.

This was Frankie's main task: making sure it was right this time. So no one would get hurt.

The rest of the morning was normal. Shower. Brush teeth. Wait at the top of the stairs until she heard her dad leave for the morning—nothing would happen if she ran into him on a bad morning, most of the time. But those other times were memorable enough to make Frankie cautious.

As soon as the front door closed, April's door swung open next to Frankie, who jolted out of the way just in time to avoid getting run over.

"Always in my waaaay," April sang at her as she headed down the stairs. She'd been waiting, too. They used to wait together, making up stories in April's bed until they heard that telltale door slam, worlds apart from how their mom closed the door: an annoyed, distracted jerk closed rather than a slam that rattled the frame.

Frankie tried to think of something witty to say while April ran down the stairs.

"Shut up," was what she finally came up with.

It was awkward. There was no other word for it. The thrill of yesterday had worn off, and Frankie stood on the step for a good five seconds before one of them thought of something to say.

Ivy went first. "What day is your test?"

Frankie had to think about it. Before yesterday she'd been considering not showing up, and accepting her fate at summer school.

"Uh, the Thursday after next."

"So we only have two weeks."

Frankie nodded. "Time limit."

Ivy's lips twitched. She ducked her head. It was cute. Frankie had to avert her gaze to stop from doing something mortifying, like blushing. All her foundation would hide it, right?

"Want to cram?"

"Don't have much of a choice." Frankie's hands flexed around her backpack. She'd finally gotten a black one last Christmas after her parents gave her a catalog and told her to get whatever she wanted for under fifty bucks. "How's your furry little problem?"

Ivy glanced back into the empty house. "Babylove's fine. I think he takes a few days to get hungry again. How's the nixing spell going?"

Frankie dug in her deep pocket for the note. "So I was thinking about this library book—"

A voice spoke up from the driveway. "Is she lost?"

Annoyance and panic in equal measure. Frankie turned around to see Marvin goddamn Martin in that stupid polo shirt—he had seven versions of the same blue shirt, like an asshole.

Ivy fluttered a hand through her straightened hair. "What are you doing here? I called you."

"I didn't see any messages. So you were...serious?" He looked pointedly at his girlfriend, confused and a little hurt he wasn't being let in on the joke.

"I was."

"Ooookay." Marvin made a face that meant *I'll go with it, but you'll tell me later.* "Gonna be an awkward walk then."

"No, I wanted..." Ivy folded her arms across her chest. No cheer uniform today, just a simple pink dress. Frills at the hem. It looked like something her parents picked out for her back in middle school. "Me and Frankie were going to go over some study stuff. Hard to do that with someone else around."

She softened it with apologetic eyes she obviously didn't

mean. Marvin kept watching her, as if trying to uncover a secret meaning behind her *very* clear words, and irritation flared in Frankie's gut again: *she wants you to go away! What's your problem?*

She waited for him to argue. For a moment it looked like he was going to. Then he clicked his tongue, spinning on his heel in one smooth motion.

"Alright," he said, the word heavy with implications. "See you at school. You too, Tanner."

"Can't wait," Frankie snapped. She watched him turn back onto the street. "Jesus, cut the cord already."

Ivy sighed. "He insists. It's sweet, really."

Frankie put more flair than usual into her eye roll.

"It's sweet," Ivy repeated, and then blinked. "I...just like having time to myself sometimes."

Frankie snorted. "Sorry to bother you, princess."

"No, come on." Ivy closed the door behind her and started down the steps. "I didn't mean..."

They walked in slow silence, putting distance between them and Marvin. When they turned onto the street, it was empty.

"I'm sorry if..." Ivy sucked in an uncharacteristically nervous breath. Everything about her was uncharacteristic these past two days—gone was the cool, confident, controlled Ivy she recognized from the hallways. In its place was this strange, stressed girl Frankie couldn't quite put her finger on.

"I'm sorry if I was a bitch to you," Ivy continued.

It was a nice thing to say. For a moment Frankie was even touched. Then she thought about school, the trajectory they were on through the old cracked streets. She thought of her sister. Ivy could apologize all she wanted, but that didn't mean she wouldn't revert straight back to cool, collected jackass once they hit those swinging doors of Bulldeen High.

"It's fine," Frankie said flatly.

Ivy startled at the venom in her tone. Scratched at the skin near her mouth, where a small red patch was forming, mostly hidden with foundation.

"Um," she said. "Anyway. You were talking about a library book?"

Right. Had to earn her keep.

"It's about resurrection myths in different cultures," Frankie started as they turned the corner. "It has some stuff about hunger, nothing on *controlling* the hunger, but—"

A shoulder collided with hers. Frankie stumbled, only managing not to fall straight on her ass thanks to Ivy's steadying hand on her arm.

"Gosh," said Babe Simmons. He hunched into his skinny shoulders, trying to shorten his tall frame. "I'm so sorry, I didn't see you!"

"We'll keep a weather eye out next time," Dude said dryly, because of course it was him. Of course Babe Simmons and Dude Marsh had been too busy staring into each other's eyes to look where they were going. They had tunnel vision like that. Frankie would be surprised the girls were in that friend group at all, if she hadn't seen how warm the boys were towards them. It wasn't that they didn't love their friends, it was just that when Babe and Dude were around each other, it was hard for anything else to leak in. For example: freshmen walking right in front of them.

Frankie flipped her fringe out of her face. It hadn't been in the way, it just looked cool.

"It's fine," she said. She jerked her head at Ivy. "Come on."

She pretended not to notice the strange look they gave her —*since when are those two hanging out?*—and made herself not look back to check the close proximity of their arms, brushing as they walked. There were no out gay people in Bulldeen, and maybe Frankie was blowing things out of proportion. But she was a closeted lesbian in small-town 2003 USA: she would clutch at whatever straws drifted her way.

Frankie looked over to Ivy, ready to keep talking about library books, only to find Ivy twisting back to watch the boys leave.

"Where are they off to? School's that way."

"Who knows? Dude and Babe have their own little world going on."

Ivy nodded, still watching them walk. Frankie chanced a glance. The boy's elbows brushed as Babe laughed. The only time Ivy thought Babe might be a fun person to know was when Dude was making him laugh. It opened him up, made him drop all that soft-spoken polite bullshit.

"They're *close*," Ivy said. She was smiling, but it was edged with something Frankie didn't like.

It struck Frankie as the sort of joke that would get thrown around in Ivy's friend group. In her *sister's* friend group.

She fussed with the buckle of her backpack so she had something to look at. "Sure are."

"Like...*very* close."

Frankie dropped the buckle and stared until Ivy's smile faded.

"Uh," Ivy said. "I didn't mean—"

Frankie cut her off. "I'm too tired for this," she said, and yawned to prove her point. It turned real halfway through, jaw cracking, eyes watering with the force of it.

It was going to be a *long* two weeks.

chapter
four

THE REST of the week passed in a haze, though not as hazily as Frankie would have liked. Ivy liked to pull her out of the cafeteria to study, so her usual pick-me-up smoke break was gone. She lasted until Friday, when she found an empty corner of the parking lot and lit up.

She waved as Ivy approached.

"Okay, so today I think we should really start focusing on —" Ivy stopped. Sniffed. Her whole face creased as she took stock of the joint Frankie was sucking on.

Frankie couldn't help the laugh, pulled out of her by that scandalized expression and a healthy dose of weed. She blew one last plume of smoke, then crushed the dregs under her boot.

"Is that—are you high at *school*? I thought that was just a rumor!" Ivy stepped close enough for Frankie to catch a whiff of her peach-scented deodorant.

"It's *after* school right now."

"Wait." Ivy frowned. "Is that—is *that* what that smell is? I thought you just took a lot of shop classes! Or—or burned incense!"

Frankie laughed again, so delighted she would've been

embarrassed to make such a sound if she were sober. "Dude, I smell like a dorm room!"

"Well, *I* didn't know what it smelled like!" Ivy said, oddly flustered. "Can you study like this?"

"I've been high every time we've studied! I'm not *wasted,* princess. It's just taking the edge off." Frankie winked. She was not a born winker, her other eye flinching in the process, but it worked well enough.

Ivy went quiet. Frankie waited for her to make another appalled comment about the weed, but she just stared, a little out of it. Contact high?

"Uh...we..." Ivy shook her head, a strand of pale hair sticking to her lipgloss. She didn't move to unstick it.

Frankie reached out. Ivy stood shock-still as Frankie unhooked the strand of hair from her mouth.

"Lipgloss," Frankie said, wiping her fingers on a bare bit of skin between her long sleeves and bracelets. The smallest smear of gloss gleamed in the eye sockets of her skull ring, but she wouldn't notice until that night, taking off her rings before bed. She'd meant to be funny, picking hair away from Ivy's lips, but suddenly it felt dangerous: stupid, risky, something that would get her in trouble.

Ivy was scarily silent so long Frankie dared to look up. Ivy startled, swiping the telltale strand behind her ear.

"Thanks," she said, her voice thin and strange. She cleared her throat. "Let's...let's just go."

The awkwardness was mostly gone by the time they walked to the Wexler house. It was weirdly easy to get banter going, and like every time they hung out, Frankie found herself caught between enjoyment and deep, primordial terror at its imminent ending. It had been so long since she'd bantered with anyone—

the closest she got was her weed guy, Thomas Jr., who was only fun to hang out with after both of them had smoked up first.

Frankie's usual malaise about Shakespeare eased when she could listen to Ivy recite it.

"It's not meant to be read," Ivy said, a fire in her eyes Frankie had never seen in her before this week, not even as a kid. "It's meant to be *performed*."

Frankie lay back on her bed. It was a double, laden with pillows, and Frankie had shoved all the pillows off her side, unlike Ivy, who had them piled up behind her back. "Perform for me!"

Ivy chuckled. "Not by *me*."

"I wanna hear you."

"Ugh." Ivy fought a smile and bent down over the textbook. "Don't laugh."

"Me? Never!"

"Shut up." Ivy grinned, and her shoulders straightened even more than usual. Her voice took on a heavy timbre. "*These violent delights have violent ends / And in their triumph die, like fire and powder / Which as they kiss consume: the sweetest honey / Is loathsome in his own deliciousness / And in the taste confounds the appetite—*"

Frankie had been planning on doing a fake snore, but she couldn't stop herself from smiling. "See? It's fun when you do it, princess. Just gotta have you stand there during the test yelling the lines."

"Lines won't help you with *themes*. Or *interpretation*. Or anything useful, except quoting." Ivy toyed with the corner of the example questions Mr. Clack had given them—part multiple choice, part mini-essay shit. Frankie had hoped for all multiple choice—if you had no idea, you still had some chance of getting it right, unlike with open questions, where you had to make something up.

Frankie twisted to check the blinking clock on the bedside table. "It's getting late. We gotta switch to dark shit."

"What? Oh." She shook the sample test. "Do you feel prepared on *Romeo and Juliet?*"

Frankie snorted. "No, but that's what the weekends are for, right?" She bent down to drag her backpack close to the bed. "Hey," she said, as she unloaded the library books she'd gotten at lunch, "why not ask Milly Hart to help with this? She reads this shit, too. I think she's even into Latin. She *definitely* knows it better than me."

Ivy gave her a *duh* look. "Because she's an adult? She has a full-time job?" She settled back into her pillow pile. "I don't know. I think she'd be hard to talk to."

Frankie guffawed. "And I'm *not*?"

"Nnnno?" Ivy adjusted her books into a neat stack. "I mean—Milly was *always* quiet and weird. You used to talk a lot, so I know you can."

Frankie ducked her head, cheeks burning. She didn't get a lot of reminders about what she was like in grade school. Everybody was embarrassing as a kid, but it still made her cringe to look back and remember how naive she used to be—it was harder to tell when people were making fun of her, back then. She'd let them string her along, gormless and stupid, until someone laughed right in her face. Only then would she catch on. Over the years she started looking out for it, watching for signs that would always, always come. She built walls and lined them with barbed wire.

So why was she blushing like an idiot in Ivy Wexler's bedroom?

Frankie busied herself with the books. She'd gotten four, each one making the librarian glare at her harder. Frankie had barely resisted the urge to flip her off on the way out. Weren't librarians meant to care about educating kids? So what if that education was about dark magic?

"So a lot of it sounds like bullshit," Frankie said, spreading open the first book. "But last week I thought all the resurrection stories around town were bullshit, and then your cat killed and ate a dog three times its size. Anyway, *obviously* a sacrifice has to be made, and it's not just the blood at the start. Stuff happens after."

"Deaths," Ivy said softly.

"Mmm."

They looked at each other. It didn't need to be said: Milly Hart. Grandma Higgins, whatever her name was. Maybe there were more. Maybe the schoolyard gossip they'd been told as children was the tip of the iceberg, and Bulldeen was even more rotten than they thought.

Ivy tugged at her wispy hair. The long hours in school made it wavy at the edges, but it still clung to straightness.

Frankie folded the page over for later. Then, because Ivy's legs were pulled up so tight into her stomach, arms cradling her knees for comfort: "Hey, are you...are you really sure you want to do this?"

"What?"

"Like, it just seems risky."

Ivy stared at her like she was missing something. "That's why I have you. We'll be fine if the nixing spell works."

"Yeah, but..." Frankie sighed. "Never mind. So what was he like, your granddad? I didn't see him around much."

She wasn't even sure of his name. Gerald, maybe. Or Geoff. Something old and white.

Ivy looked away, a smile tugging her lips. "He was great. Smart. Funny. Really passionate. He's the one who taught me about Shakespeare. If you think I make it fun, you should've seen him."

"Passionate," Frankie repeated. She didn't know the Wexlers well, but until today she wouldn't have described any of them like that. The Wexlers were a prim, polite bunch with razor edges. When Frankie was seven, she'd bumped into Mrs. Wexler in the street, spilling her groceries, and the hard smile she got in return was so withering Frankie ran home crying.

Ivy nodded. "Everybody said it was an age thing. He used to be way more put together. But by the time I knew him, he was just...great. Always laughing the loudest. Charismatic. He wanted me to be an actor, before..."

"Before?"

"Nothing. Turned out I wasn't that good at it, so I stopped." Ivy's troubled expression cleared, forcibly wiped clean. "So why are you failing? You're smart."

"Says who?"

"Me." Ivy nodded down at all the occult books. "Plus you're always reading. How are you failing English?"

Frankie groaned. She thought she was done with this interrogation. She'd never been a great student, so teachers didn't lean on her very hard when her mediocre grades started spiraling into downright failure.

"It's just so boring," she whined. "Who cares what all these old dead guys have to say?"

"I thought you'd be into some of that stuff—all their long, dark monologuing."

"Not when *they* do it."

"Kafka. Dorian Gray."

"Dorian Gray is cool." Frankie wiped her sweaty palms surreptitiously on her ripped jeans. She'd always thought that book was about a gay relationship, but the one time she brought it up in class everyone, including the teacher, looked at her like she was the biggest freak in the world.

"Some bits of Kafka are fun. But you gotta sift through all

that shit to get it." Frankie twisted her rings, grating them against each other to hear the metallic rasp. "I'm gonna light up. Okay if I do it out your window?"

"Okay," Ivy said, sounding much less scandalized than earlier. "Just don't let the smoke get—"

"Got it." Frankie walked over and pushed the window open. She dug the lighter from one of her endless pockets, a rolled joint from the other one.

"Very prepared," Ivy muttered.

"Girl scout motto, baby." Frankie lit up, all too aware of Ivy's gaze burning a hole in the back of her dyed hair. She put extra effort into pursing her dark mouth around the cigarette, inhaling slow and steady, breathing out in one smooth stream. She'd only started smoking two years ago, but she'd had a lot of practice.

A comforting blanket wrapped around the jagged bits of Frankie's mind. She closed her eyes, savoring it. In the first few moments of a joint—if she got lucky, anyway—nothing could touch her.

"Can I try some?"

Frankie choked. "Two hours ago you were freaking out, and now you want some?"

"I was freaking out over you being high at *school*. It's *school*!" Ivy held out a hand.

Frankie blew a trail of smoke out the window. "What happened to *don't get smoke in my room*?"

Ivy's blue eyes widened. She got up and joined Frankie at the window, their shoulders brushing. Ivy's hand came out in a stiff peace sign.

Frankie fitted the joint into it. Tiny, callused fingers. Bitten nails. Ivy had tried to file it out, make it less obvious, but there were those tiny telltale marks. Almost imperceptible red dots where teeth worried the skin. Up this close Frankie could more clearly see the dark worry spot next to Ivy's mouth where she liked to rub. Frankie thought about twisting her rings. Bruised apples. Pressing her fingers hard into Ivy's jaw, watching it turn red, then deep purple.

"Just like a cigarette," Frankie said when she realized Ivy was waiting for instruction. "You *have* smoked a cigarette, right?"

"I'm not twelve." Ivy breathed in gently. Frankie waited for her to cough, but Ivy just kept breathing, one long inhale, then turned towards the open window and breathed out. "It tastes weird."

"You get used to it."

Ivy took another careful hit. Frankie opened her mouth to make fun of her, but the words died in her throat. The moment felt strangely tender, a soap bubble she didn't want to break. It had been so long since she'd stood this close to someone.

Ivy handed the joint back. Red gloss prints decorated the base. Frankie set her mouth over them.

Ivy looked up at her, pupils not yet huge. "Can I try your lipstick?"

Frankie felt herself nod. Ivy walked towards the bed and Frankie thought: *not something to happen in front of the windows.*

Frankie stubbed out the joint and joined her at the edge of the bed. Dug her trademark lipstick out of her endless pockets. Ivy took it and wiped off her lipgloss.

"*Graveyard Dark,*" she read out.

Frankie nodded. "It's the only black lipstick they sell in Bulldeen. I got it from the chemist."

Ivy held it out.

Frankie uncapped it, rolling the tube in her fingers. It grated against her rings. She wanted to run. She wanted to sit here forever, knees touching on the pink mattress, Ivy tilting her face towards her, lips bare and parted. Waiting.

"Stay still," Frankie said uselessly, and leaned in.

Ivy's bottom lip twitched under that first cool touch. Frankie followed the bow of her lips, going over once, twice. A third time, just to be sure.

A crimson flush sat high on Ivy's cheeks. "Grab me a tissue?"

Frankie took one from the bedside table and put it between Ivy's lips. Ivy pressed into it, and Frankie thought of grade school, trying on her mom's makeup with—who was it? It had to be April, it made sense if it was April, but she didn't think it had been.

Black marks on the tissue. Frankie crumpled it, thinking of those black marks transferring to her hand, thinking of applying lipstick next time, the warmth transferring from Ivy's mouth to the lipstick to Frankie's mouth—could that happen?

Ivy stared. Her eyes were moons.

Frankie couldn't breathe. "What?"

"Do I look good?"

A dark smile. It didn't dull her. If anything, it made everything else look brighter.

Frankie nodded. *We match*, she wanted to say, but she couldn't make herself speak. The soap bubble grew tighter and tighter, and any movement might burst it.

Ivy leaned in—

A shriek cut the world in half.

Frankie jerked backwards, sliding off the bed.

"Shit," Ivy said. "What—"

Another scream. This one sounded human. Agonized. Childlike.

"Oh *god*." Ivy bolted, only stopping to grab Frankie and haul her up. Both of them stumbled and then sprinted out the door, down the steps and into the evening, where the screaming was getting louder.

They were still running when the gunshot rang out.

Frankie jumped. Ivy just sped up. The yells were coming from a house at the end of the block. The gate was still latched —no one else had come out to check.

Ivy threw the latch open and ran down the side of the house. No screams anymore, just crying.

Ivy skidded to a stop. Frankie almost ran into her.

Babylove was dead, for good this time. His head was open, blood and brains sprawling over the grass. An unmoving paw still stretched out towards the hysterical toddler in his mother's iron grip, his pudgy arm bleeding heavily.

The mother's head flew up. Tears stained Maura Gracegood's cheeks, face warped with horror. A shotgun lay at her side, the acrid stench of powder still in the air.

"You," she spat at Ivy, clutching her child closer. "Is this *thing*—is this your cat?"

"I'm so sorry," Ivy cried. "Is he okay?"

"Does he LOOK okay?" Maura screamed. She wobbled up from the ground, hugging her toddler to her chest. Richie Gracegood continued to scream. He didn't know pain like this existed. Nothing bad had happened to Richie until today.

"Crazy thing ran out of nowhere," Maura sobbed as she ran inside, emerging shortly with the car keys. "You should've —should lock that thing up—"

"I'm sorry," Ivy repeated. "I'm so sorry, I hope he's alright..."

"Can we help?" Frankie asked weakly.

Maura ignored them as she buckled Richie into the car seat, tying a mostly-clean dishtowel around his bleeding arm.

Only while climbing into the driver's seat did she look at the girls again, hands trembling on the steering wheel.

"He was a nice cat," she croaked. It was not a *sorry*. "I used to feed him snacks. He'd sit on the windowsill."

"He *was* a nice cat," Ivy whispered, eyes wet. Her mouth wobbled, and Frankie remembered, oh, right, the re-death of her family cat might actually affect her.

A renewed cry made them all flinch.

Maura twisted towards the back seat. "It's okay, sweetie, everything's going to be okay!"

The car lurched down the driveway. Frankie and Ivy watched it peel around the corner, then stood there until the engine faded into silence. It took a while. Bulldeen streets were quiet and empty, and sound traveled.

Frankie turned reluctantly towards the bloodstained ground. Babylove's blank eyes stared at nothing, his white fur stained shocking red. He looked almost pitiful like this.

Ivy's lipstick was smudged. Frankie didn't know when it had happened. The soap bubble in the bedroom felt like it happened weeks ago.

In the distance, a siren wailed.

five

CHIEF KATE HIGGINS was as useless as ever, and Frankie had never been so grateful.

She didn't say anything during their stammered explanation of rabies. She took one look at the bloody yard and asked if they were going to clean that up, or if they'd get Maura to do it.

After some mumbling, the girls said they'd do it.

And that was it.

"Do it fast or it'll start to stink." Chief Higgins adjusted her belt and got back in her car.

They buried Babylove in his old grave at the back of the Wexlers' yard.

"At least you don't have to explain to your parents why he's up and about again," Frankie said.

Ivy just scrubbed harder under her nails. She'd been the one to drag the cat into the plastic bag, and she'd held it open for Frankie to shovel the bloody dirt on top of it. They didn't know any other way to clean a backyard. They left a ragged scoop in the grass. Better than blood, Frankie reasoned.

Ivy's black lipstick—*Frankie's* black lipstick—had all but evaporated from Ivy's mouth by the time she dried her hands. She'd spent a lot of the last half hour with her lips pressed tightly together, face white, trying not to puke at the literal brains they were scooping into a Shop N' Save bag.

"The next one will go better," Frankie said as she stood on the front steps. "We'll make sure of it."

Ivy gave an unconvincing smile.

Frankie turned to leave.

"Um," Ivy said. "Just so you know. The ritual—the nixing spell part, there's more."

Frankie turned back slowly. "And you waited until now to say it? I'm precaution girl. *Safety* girl. I need to know all the details to be safety girl."

"I know, I just..." Ivy rubbed the spot near her mouth, then wrenched her hand down. "I didn't want to talk about it."

"It?"

"The thing, whatever it was. I think the nixing spell is about taking its power away. I think *it* causes the hunger." Ivy's face tightened, retreating down and down inside herself until Frankie could barely see her.

Then she snapped back, swallowing thickly. "It—it showed up the night Babylove came back. I went into the basement, and it was there, standing over his cage. For a second I thought my granddad was back, but it wasn't...it *wasn't*. He was too sharp, too tall, it was wearing this old coat Granddad would never touch. And he—*it*—smiled at me. Its teeth were sharp, and then they weren't."

Frankie nodded. She made sure her voice wouldn't squeak as she said, "And?"

"And...that's it."

"What, he walked out of your basement?"

"No, it vanished. Like—" Ivy motioned. *Poof.* "And it said something before it went? I don't know what it meant."

"Ivy! You're killing me with the pauses! What did he say?"

"Nothing! It just said, 'it hadn't been an animal before',

that it was 'interesting,' and that he 'looked forward to watching what happened.'"

Frankie shivered. She should call bullshit. She should call animal control, tell them about a rabies-infested cat, and yell at Ivy for messing with her. But something deep inside her *knew*. It didn't feel like discovery. It felt like uncovering something she'd lost a long time ago, something she'd buried. *Are you sure you want to do this?* She wanted to ask it, over and over again, until Ivy gave her the answer she wanted.

"Cryptic," Frankie whispered.

Ivy nodded, wrapping her arms around herself. She'd never looked so small, standing on the porch in the evening light.

"We'll be fine if we get the nixing spell right," she said. "Then it can't do anything. It can't make the hunger."

Frankie nodded. She wanted to ask more. She wanted to run home and hide. She wanted to ask if Ivy was waking up in cold sweats, too, filled with fear from dreams she couldn't remember.

What she said was: "See you tomorrow."

When Frankie emerged, tragically sober, into the cafeteria the next day, Ivy was sitting at her table in her cheerleading uniform.

Frankie stood in the entrance for a while, weighing up her options. She told herself she was freaked out about the cat re-murder, about the not-guy in the basement, which she was. But all she could think of at that moment was Ivy in her black lipstick.

It probably wasn't even going to be a kiss, Frankie reasoned. She was going to whisper a secret in Frankie's ear, or something. Bite her? Biting felt more likely than kissing. Kissing wasn't a thing that happened to Frankie.

"Hello," Ivy said, scribbling distractedly on a card as Frankie sat down across from her. "I wrote you some flashcards." She tapped the stack until the cards settled into place. "Do you want to start with *Romeo and Juliet* or *The Tempest*?"

Frankie looked around. A few people were staring, obviously. Marvin wasn't, but he had his suspiciously unmoving back to them in a way that meant he was doing his absolute darndest to listen in.

Ivy rapped the cards impatiently against the table. "Hello? *Romeo and Juliet* or *The Tempest*?"

Frankie blinked. "*Tempest.*"

"I was afraid you'd say that."

"Boring, right? Even more than usual." Frankie allowed herself a sly smile. "Think you can make it interesting for me? Do some Prospero in the middle of the cafeteria?"

Ivy barked a high-pitched laugh. Gaspy. Real. Loud enough that Marvin's head whipped around, eyebrows drawn in like that one eagle muppet. He wasn't the only one to look —people from other tables, including Babe Simmons, glanced over, gazes sticking when they noticed who was laughing together.

Ivy covered the gaspy laugh with a cough. "Uh, maybe not." Her gaze turned self-conscious as she looked around the cafeteria, all those eyes on her.

Frankie clenched her jaw, shoving down the betrayal. *You have nothing to be betrayed,* she reminded herself. *This was always a temporary thing.*

"I'm sorry, want to call me a freak to make up for that? I can spit at you if you want. Really help the performance."

"Spit?" Ivy's face twisted, and for a second they were exactly who they had been last week: antagonistic strangers who had once hugged behind the swings.

The cards clicked once more against the table, a tidy stack

adorned with loopy handwriting. "Who are the main charac-
ters of the Tempest, and how do they each tie into the play's
core themes?"

The rest of lunch was a slow, boring slide. Every time
Frankie tried to pry something fun out of Ivy, she would only
receive a twitch or a look in return. This wasn't helped by
Frankie getting meaner the less reaction she got.

"I'm just trying to help," Ivy hissed as the lunch period
drew to a close.

"You're being *boring*. If you really wanted me to learn,
you'd get up on the table and start monologuing!"

"You are so—"

The bell rang. Frankie and Ivy glowered at each other.

"Baby?" Marvin appeared at Ivy's shoulder, doing his best
to ignore Frankie, who was doing the same right back at him.
"We need to get to Gym."

"I know," Ivy snarled.

Marvin spluttered.

Ivy sat up straight as if a switch had been flipped. She
scratched the spot next to her mouth, which grew redder every
day. Soon she would break the skin.

"I'm sorry," she said. "Frankie is being difficult."

"*Someone's* being difficult," Frankie muttered.

"Shocker," Marvin said over her. He covered Ivy's shoulder
with his meaty palm. "Anyway, time to go."

Ivy stood. Her cheerleading skirt swished at her knees,
barely long enough for the school board not to come after her
for it. Frankie stubbornly did not look at her thighs.

Ivy walked at Marvin's side. Frankie watched her go,
contemplating ditching next period altogether to smoke up in
the bathrooms, or even head home.

Halfway to the door, Ivy turned. Stalked back up to
Frankie, bending down so their noses almost touched. Frankie,

who had been about to come up with an angry retort, fell silent, rocked by the sudden proximity. The lightest freckles adorned Ivy's nose underneath the makeup.

Ivy bared her teeth. "If you spit on me, I'll spit right back."

The smallest smile. Then she was gone, swishing back to her confused boyfriend, not looking back over her shoulder as Frankie giggled. It was a noise nobody had heard from her for years, a noise so rare everyone passing stopped to watch it happen: Loser Tanner, giggling like a little kid because of Ivy Wexler.

She was still smiling to herself at the end of English when Mr. Clack waved her over. He was one of the teachers who actually cared about his students, so he noticed and was shocked by her uncharacteristic smile.

"Did something nice happen today?"

Frankie shrugged. She liked Mr. Clack, but she wasn't about to spill her soul to him.

He beamed at her. He was forty-three. He was a kind, stubborn, soft-spoken man who genuinely wanted what was best for others to an extent that pissed off many adults and all teenagers. His only friend was his terrier, Snufkins.

"Glad to hear it! I hope this adds to the pile."

Frankie narrowed her eyes at him. "Hope what adds to the pile?"

He handed her a piece of paper. Frankie took it. It was the homework she'd dropped into his cubby this morning, two days after its due date. In clear red writing, Mr. Clack had scribbled *C+*.

"That's a C," Frankie said.

He tapped the paper. "C *plus*! I told you you'd get ahead if you just put the work in."

Frankie traced the letter reverently. "That was fast. I've only been studying a week. I mean I've been studying the whole time," she amended, when Mr. Clack's face tightened.

She sighed. "I did *try* to study."

"Well, something's obviously started to click." Mr. Clack made a motion like he was going to pat her shoulder, then dropped his hand. "Keep it up! Knew I was right to offer you that make-up test."

Frankie walked away from the nicest interaction with a teacher she'd had since grade school with a low buzzing in her stomach. It was unfamiliar, and she took a moment to identify it as hope.

She strode into the hall, right into Ivy.

"*Watch* it—" Ivy's face cleared. "Whoa, what's with you?"

Frankie held up the paper, trying and failing to hide her smile.

Ivy did the same, pushing them close to the lockers so they could have the conversation out of the way of the crowd bustling to the next class. "That's a big improvement, right?"

"Yes!"

"Great!" They stood there staring at each other, and it occurred to Frankie that Ivy might hug her. It occurred to Frankie she might want to be hugged. It was a mortifying realization, and the next one was worse: Ivy would never hug her in public.

Frankie clenched her teeth until her smile was under control. "So—still on for the ritual next Sunday?"

Ivy shushed her. "I think so. We're cutting it a little close, my parents are back the next day—but I want to be really prepared. Do you think you have the translation right?"

"I think so," Frankie said. She thought again about asking if Ivy was having weird dreams. Ever since she went over to Ivy's house she would wake up in a panic, sheets soaked in sweat. The only thing she could remember from her dreams was white fur, scratching, something trying to get out—or maybe in? Sometimes she had tears on her face. On those mornings, she was left with this deep, terrible hole, like she'd lost something hugely important.

But the feeling never lasted longer than a shower, and Ivy was so beautiful under the fluorescent lights, and the happy buzz was still in her stomach, so big and so buzzy it swallowed the dark knot of unease that had been growing ever since Ivy said *resurrection*.

chapter
six

IT WAS their last full weekend before the time limit ran out. They'd cram for the ritual on Saturday, then on Sunday they'd cram for the make-up test. The closer the resurrection date came, the redder the patch near Ivy's mouth grew. It was hard to know what was helpful and what was bullshit when their one definite example was buried—permanently—in the back-yard. Frankie tried to talk to Milly Hart, but the woman started wheezing, genuinely fearful, until Frankie gave up and walked off.

They were pretty sure they could avoid the bloodlust. Though, Frankie admitted, it would be hilarious seeing Granddad Wexler lunge for the clerk's throat during his morning grocery trip.

"That's not funny," Ivy told her.

Frankie shrugged. Their shoulders grazed. They were lying the wrong way on Ivy's bed, feet dangling near the endless pillows. Frankie had shoved hers onto Ivy's side, so Ivy's feet were elevated to a ridiculous degree.

Frankie tucked her chin into her hands. "Tell me more about him. Granddad Wexler."

Ivy looked at the wall. They had yellow wallpaper, the same

sickly shade as most of the houses in Bulldeen. Even when they escaped Bulldeen, the girls would be equal parts comforted and repulsed whenever they saw it in other houses.

"Like what?"

"I don't know. Whatever."

Ivy hummed. She was wearing a thin hoodie, the most casual thing Frankie had ever seen her in. Before today, Frankie didn't know Ivy *owned* a hoodie.

"He liked albatrosses. He liked that long poem about the dead one. He hated carrots but loved carrot cake. He could guess any song if you hummed it. Once, he caught me smoking and he made me smoke the whole pack."

"Ew. Did you—"

"Puke? Yeah."

"Ew," Frankie repeated. "Mean."

"No, it worked. Other than that time with the lipstick, I haven't smoked since." She fussed at a hangnail with her teeth. Red bloomed beneath her teeth. "He's going to be mad I didn't get him back sooner."

"At least you're doing it! Why didn't your family get in on this?"

"Oh, that kind of talk isn't...allowed. You know? All that dark Bulldeen gossip. My dad says it's crap, but I think he's scared."

Frankie thought of blood drenching that white fur, that cute little collar slick with it. The collar was still around Babylove's neck when they dumped him unceremoniously back into his grave.

"It was one of the only things they fought about," Ivy continued, rubbing a blonde strand of hair between her slim fingers. "Granddad joked about it sometimes, and Dad would shut him down. Everybody was afraid he wasn't joking."

"When did he tell you he wasn't?"

"I knew the whole time." Ivy's strong jaw flexed in the weak evening light. "When I was a kid he'd tell me I had a very important job. That his friend had given him the key to immortality—"

"Holy shit!" Frankie laughed loudly enough that Ivy twisted to glare at her.

"It's a big deal!"

"I know, I'm just imagining this old guy sitting down this kid like—" Frankie waggled her hands in front of her face like the wizard in the one and only traveling circus that had stopped in Bulldeen. "Baaah! Resurrect me, child!"

She'd been seven years old when the circus came to town. The circus posters said they were staying for a week, but when Frankie tried to get April to take her back, they'd walked into an empty lawn. When they asked where the circus had gone, they'd been told they up and left in the middle of the night. *They got spooked*, the adults said. *Out of towners always get spooked in Bulldeen.*

"I did think it might be a joke, when I got a bit older." Ivy worried at her thumb, at those impossibly short nails. "But...I don't know. He wouldn't lie about something that big. Besides, there's just something *about* Bulldeen."

"Bad place," Frankie whispered. "Unnatural."

Ivy whipped around, blue eyes wide in recognition. She opened and closed her mouth, a wrinkle in her plucked brow.

"Yes," she said finally. "That."

"Someone said that to you, too?"

"I think so?"

"Who?"

Ivy rubbed the red patch. "I don't know."

Frankie shivered. Ivy sat up and handed her a pillow.

"Thanks." Frankie hugged it to her chest. It was one of

those fuzzy heart pillows, faded with age. Frankie felt obligated to send Ivy a judgy look as she hugged it.

"Shut up. I got most of these as a kid."

"When your granddad was giving you resurrection instructions."

"He didn't actually let me see the ritual until I was twelve."

"Oh, when you were *twelve*. That's fine then."

The ritual sat folded on the bedside table. Frankie stretched out a bare foot, skimming the corner with her toes. He'd kept it under his mattress, Ivy had told her. Decades of that man's weight at night. April used to warn Frankie that if you kept a story under your pillow, it would seep into your mind and set up roots. It'd make the story *real*. It was a tactic to get Frankie to stop reading scary books before bed and having to climb into April's later, but it just made Frankie shove her favorite books under her pillow, wishing for a group of friends or a boarding school or a secret set of parents to take her and April away.

"What'd Granddad do for a living?"

Ivy sighed. "Take a guess."

"Thornfruit factory?"

"Uh-huh. Packaging." Thornfruit fields surrounded Bulldeen on three out of four sides, and the factory employed a good portion of the town's population. Thornfruit was spiky, green and disgusting, and the only reason Bulldeen was still around after all this time. It lived off the poison in the soil left over from the dump that was once located on this land. Once the poison was leached dry, the thornfruit crops would die. Bulldeen would die with it.

In Frankie's opinion, it couldn't happen fast enough.

"Bane of his existence," she continued. "He hated it there. Hated this whole town. But he got mad when I said I didn't like it."

"That's weird."

"No, it's sweet. He wanted me to stay in Bulldeen."

"Didn't he care about what you wanted?"

Ivy's brow furrowed.

"You don't get it," she said. "I was, like...his *person*. He needed me. I knew all his secrets."

"Did he know all of yours?"

Ivy stared at her. Her eyes were moons again. Frankie's heart twisted.

The moment stretched. Frankie meant to look away. *Any second now*, she told herself, *Ivy will look away and the moment will end. Enjoy it while it lasts.*

Freckles on Ivy's nose, barely visible. Frankie itched to touch them.

She reached up—

The phone rang. Ivy startled. She lunged over Frankie to grab it from the table, and Frankie held her breath as Ivy's hair brushed her cheek.

"Sorry," Ivy said.

"No, it's fine." Frankie pressed a hand over her chest, calming her heart.

Ivy leaned back with the phone. "Hello?"

Marvin's voice oozed from the speaker. "What time am I coming over tonight?"

Right. Frankie dropped her head back against the mattress. The *party*.

"Everybody's coming at nine, so. Nine."

"Yeah, but do you need help setting up?"

Ivy stilled. Frankie could only see her back; she'd twisted away when she realized it was Marvin.

"That's...really sweet of you."

"I'm a sweet guy."

Frankie mimed vomiting.

Ivy, back turned, didn't notice. "It's just a house party. People will bring stuff. I just need to clear the tables out of the living room, and F—" She hesitated. "I'm all set. Thanks."

A long pause. "Is Frankie there?"

"I told you, we're cramming."

"Uh-huh. You know, you still haven't told me what you're getting out of this."

Ivy's shoulders hunched. Frankie watched the bones shift under her skin through her flimsy hoodie.

"Um," Ivy said. "Just. It's..."

Frankie sat up and grabbed the phone, making static noises into it and then slamming the END button.

Ivy's newly free hand twitched. "Excuse *you*."

"I'm *so* sorry. Just excited for my first proper house party."

Ivy's offense—mostly fake, partly real—was lost in sudden excitement. "Wait, you haven't—?"

"My last party was a birthday in grade school. No proper party shit going on there." Frankie paused. "Am I invited?"

"You're already *here*."

"I know, but..." Frankie trailed off. She hadn't considered the logistics, and based on the fading smile on Ivy's face, she hadn't either. What would Frankie do at a house party? Hang out with the stoners? Play beer pong? Neither of them could imagine hanging out like this at a party, the two of them sitting this close, having a conversation this fond in public.

Ivy plastered on an unconvincing smile. Frankie hated looking at it.

"You're invited," she said, and eased off the bed. "I need to get dressed."

There was a reason Frankie didn't get invited to house parties: no one wanted her around. And obviously she didn't want to be around any of them. It was a soul-grinding experience being stuck with these people sober during the day, let alone drunk at night. The only good thing about her classmates' increasing intoxication levels was they stopped staring at her so much. Stopped whispering. *Who invited Loser Tanner?*

"Two people invited me," she snapped back finally. "Ivy *and* Marvin invited me. He yelled it in the cafeteria, remember? Everybody heard it!"

One of the staring boys mumbled something about that being a joke, the other about not having the same lunch period.

Frankie stalked off to find some weed. She'd been looking all night, and the only person holding was Kendall J., who cut his supply with oregano. She was running out of options, except one: intimidation.

She went outside to the smokers sprawled out across the backyard, peering around for a target. *Aha.* Moe Stafford was alone, leaning up against a tree. Moe was in the year above her. He was an asshole, but his most damning trait was his choice in friends: he hung out with the most dangerous kids in school, clinging to their safety like a limpet.

Moe sniggered when he saw who it was. "Can I help you, Tanner?"

Frankie glowered. Moe immediately shrank under it. It didn't take a lot to freak out Moe Stafford when he didn't have his thorny friends with him.

"Just joking around," Moe mumbled.

A peal of laughter, familiar and awful. Frankie turned involuntarily, like a string was pulling her, to watch Ivy spin in a circle. Marvin was spinning her near the beer pong table, which they'd set up under the back porch. The porch light illuminated Ivy's blonde hair, the white dress she'd changed into, turning her into a glowing creature of light.

Frankie's chest tightened. She turned back to Moe, holding out a hand. Moe drew the joint protectively against his chest.

"Come on." Frankie motioned impatiently. "Or I hit you."

Moe sniggered again, less confidently than last time. "No, you won't."

Frankie's fist raised.

"Wait, no, don't—" Moe shoved the joint into her hand.

"Thank you." Frankie strode off, sucking smoke until it burned. *Don't look at her. Don't look.* She almost made it.

"Ayyyy, it's Loser Tanner!" Marvin's voice pierced through the dull thump of music leaking from the house. "Holy shit, she actually came. That's so *sad*! Hey, come play beer pong with us!"

Frankie turned around, considering stubbing out the joint on his neck. It was a fast decision: she wasn't about to waste what tasted like decent weed. Maybe when she smoked it to a nub.

"Gee," she said, keeping her voice dry and resolutely not looking at the girl beside him. "You make it sound so tempting."

Marvin lurched around the table to slap her shoulder. "Aw, come on! I bet you don't get to play much. Just one game, we'll let you win."

Frankie flashed her teeth. "Don't touch me."

Marvin laughed. He wasn't the only one, footballers and cheerleaders alike giggling all over each other at the show. Frankie was glad April wasn't there. She wouldn't be able to handle her sister joining in. Ivy was bad enough, standing there like a carving of a Greek goddess Frankie used to know the name of.

She didn't realize she was staring until Ivy looked up.

There, in the depths of her stomach: hope. Stupid, pitiful hope that Ivy would *do* something. Prove that their odd weeks together had actually happened, that Ivy really had leaned in with black lipstick, that Frankie made her laugh, *really* laugh, gasping with it.

Ivy's heart-shaped mouth parted. Shiny red gloss, which suited her less and less the more Frankie looked at it. That gloss had left marks on the joint they'd shared. Frankie still had it, secreted away in the bottom of her sock drawer. She took it out sometimes, turning it over in her fingers to examine the dry shine, sparkly fragments of the best and strangest thing that had ever happened to her.

Marvin's hand on her shoulder again. "Oh my god, you actually think you guys are *friends*? She's using you for weed, or whatever the hell she's getting out of you—"

Frankie shoved his hand off, but Marvin just moved in closer.

"You really are pathetic," he grated, movements loose with booze, eyes bright with tears. Desperate, Frankie realized. He needed to believe he was telling the truth, and the longer he spoke, the more he believed. "Honestly, I was fine sitting back to watch the show, but someone really has to let you down easy. Right, baby?"

Ivy averted her gaze. Her hand came up, rubbing the patch near her mouth. Even the foundation couldn't hide it now, the skin dry and scaly and dark red.

Marvin didn't seem bothered by his girlfriend's lack of participation. He leered at Frankie. "It's sad, watching you drooling over her at lunch. Almost makes me think you want—"

Frankie punched him.

Marvin fell back against the beer pong table. Cups rocked over, spilling down his pants as a chorus of gasps rose from around them, classmates stepping back as they remembered yes, this was the same girl who played with knives in the parking lot.

Marvin panted, hand hovering over his split eyebrow. Blood ran into his eye. She'd gotten him with the skull ring.

His face twisted. "You—you *bitch*! What the fuck is wrong with you?"

"WHAT'S WRONG WITH *YOU*?" Frankie screamed. She looked up one last time—stupid, *pathetic* hope—to Ivy, who was still and silent as she stared at her boyfriend's bleeding face.

Frankie stormed off. Slammed the porch door in her class-mate's faces. Charged through the house, which she knew well enough by now: she knew the trick to turning on the bathroom tap, knew that the front door stuck in the humidity, knew they had family dinners and no one said anything important or real the whole damn time, because Ivy told her about it.

Blood rushed in her ears. Scratching in the back of her head. Scratching like a cat at a door, wanting to get let in, something horrible crawling out of her dreams—

"Frankie!"

Frankie whirled. They were at the end of the driveway, Ivy running up in heels she'd complained about hours earlier as they lay on her bed. *I only wear them if I know I won't have to run anywhere*, she had said. Bad call.

"Just come back inside," Ivy coaxed. "I'll tell them not to bother you again."

She touched the inside of Frankie's elbow, over the awful stick-and-poke tattoo Frankie had revealed several days earlier. She'd said Ivy could laugh, and Ivy had said *laugh at what*, face twitching with effort not to laugh at the lumpy dolphin.

Frankie wrenched her arm away. "Why do you hang out with those assholes?"

Ivy wrung her hands. She still hadn't told Frankie where

she got the calluses. "You know how it is—small town, you grow up together—you fall into things!"

"Do you even LIKE them?"

"Sometimes," Ivy whispered.

Frankie felt the words climb her throat. She tried to swallow them back, but the options were, say the words or start crying, and she would rather take on Babylove than cry in front of anyone.

"Are we going to be friends after this week?"

Ivy made a low sound in her throat. Like a sob, like a trapped animal.

Cry or say it, Frankie thought.

Ivy did neither.

Warm mouth. Tiny hands on her face. Peach scented deodorant and the barely-there stench of burn where Ivy had held the hair straightener against her fringe for too long.

Frankie had never been kissed before. It was the sweetest, softest, most terrible feeling in the world.

Ivy pulled back with a ragged gasp and wet cheeks. She stared at Frankie with a face so open Frankie could watch as each emotion bled through: terror, dread, deep want.

"I'm..." Ivy said, and glanced around. No one looking out the windows, no one passing on the street. Their hidden little world at the end of the driveway. It didn't make either of them feel any safer.

Frankie fumbled at her wrist. "Hey."

Ivy ran. Her hand slipped from Frankie's grasp.

Frankie stood there for a long time, hand folding around empty air, getting used to the sensation of having nothing beneath it.

chapter
seven

FRANKIE DIDN'T TALK to anyone for the next three days.

A personal record. She usually only made it to two.

Sunday was easiest, huddling under the covers and sneaking into the kitchen for supplies, chain-smoking out the window until she ran out of cigarettes. School wasn't much harder—nodding during roll call, not raising her hand during class, not biting back when someone bumped into her in the hall. The last bump was an accident, Jules Havelock—the most interesting and fashionable of the dead freaks—in the middle of an apology before she trailed off. She looked more curious than nervous, which was strange, since everyone else who'd noticed the collision was steering clear. Everyone had heard about her assaulting Marvin on Saturday night.

"...sorry," Jules finished, false lashes fluttering under her purple eyeshadow. Frankie would never tell her that everyone who called her fat like it was a bad thing were idiots for not appreciating the stretch of Jules's skirt over her big thighs; that she looked forward to Jules's new outfits and her morning announcements on the PA. Under the right circumstances, Frankie might've told Jules she appreciated her for never treating Frankie like a freak. But she was on a not talking streak, and they'd never said more than a few words to each other, and people streamed around them in the hall.

Frankie shrugged. Jules swished back into the crowd.

On Wednesday, she ran into Ivy in the parking lot. This was during lunch, which Frankie had been spending flipping her knife around. She was already in trouble from doing it in the cafeteria. She was pacing, about to perfect a particularly tricky flip, when Ivy walked around the corner and right into her.

"Jesus—" Frankie stumbled, skidded, would have fallen if not for Ivy's hand on her arm. It was gone before Frankie could straighten up properly.

Ivy didn't meet her eyes. "You fall over a lot."

Frankie tried to think of something, anything, to say. Words pulled up from deep in her body.

"Not lately," she managed.

Ivy smiled thinly. The red patch near her mouth was scabbing. Then she was gone, walking fast towards the main building.

Three words. That night, she said another eight. She was in the middle of sneaking down to the kitchen for a nine p.m. slice of cheese, only to find April already had her head in the fridge, eating the best ones.

Frankie crept away.

"Hold it," April said. She closed the fridge. Like many families, the Tanners could identify each other by their footsteps. "Why are you being even freakier than usual?"

Frankie flipped her off and moved for the stairs. Something hit her in the back of the head.

Frankie bent down, peeling a cheese slice off the floor and wrinkling her nose. She threw it at April's feet.

"What went down at the party?"

Frankie glared.

"Shit, alright." April held up her hands. "Go around punching dudes, who cares? Just don't do it at school, they really want an excuse to expel you."

Frankie thought about bringing up the knife spinning in the cafeteria, but she was too tired. Let them expel her. It'd be a reason to get out of Bulldeen faster. No matter what happened, she was getting out. Of that much, she was sure.

Frankie moved again for the stairs.

"Hey—"

"Leave me alone," Frankie spat. "It's what you're best at."

The walk up to her bedroom was silent. Frankie told herself she preferred it that way. She curled under her sheets, cradled the headphones to her head and waited for the soothing tones of Linkin Park to lull her to sleep.

Thursday morning was warm and cloudy. Frankie showed up an hour early to the eight a.m. make-up exam. She'd told herself she'd cram, but instead she stood in the parking lot and twisted her rings. She didn't have any allowance money left, and there were no cigarettes in the house to steal. So that left her rings, twisted so vigorously and repeatedly Frankie worried about chafing.

She dug her nail into the eye sockets of her skull ring and shuddered. Last night's dream was harder to shake, though she could only recall glimpses: a shard of light in a dark room. Yowling. Something scrabbling at the door. At first it was a cat, but then the sound changed, becoming slow, measured. Fingers: that was the most solid thing Frankie remembered. Impossibly long, wizened fingers creeping under the door, curling up towards the knob, a scaly hand trying to let itself in.

Another shudder. Maybe it was a good thing the ritual wouldn't go ahead. Ivy wouldn't do it without Frankie. Right?

She was brought on for safety reasons. To translate the nixing spell. To be there during the ritual, and after.

I want you to be there, Ivy had said. *In case it doesn't want to 'just watch' this time.*

What do you want me to do, Frankie had asked. *Tackle it?*

Argue, Ivy replied. *Stand up to it. You're good at that.*

Like hell. Frankie's Don't Touch Me act was just that—an act, ready to fall apart at the lightest touch. After all, look what Ivy had done to her with just two weeks, study sessions, and a foray into the occult. Two weeks of talking, of sitting across from her at lunch, of knees brushing as they lay next to each other on her bed. One stolen kiss in the dark. *One* kiss, and Frankie was ruined.

She wasn't strong. She wasn't badass. What the hell could she do against the thing that appeared in Ivy's basement?

A car pulled up. Frankie watched Mr. Clack climb out of the car, wiping sleep from his eyes. He caught sight of Frankie and jumped.

"God! You're—" He checked his watch. "*Very* early. Can't wait to get the show on the road?"

Frankie cleared her throat. Her voice was rusty with disuse. "Can't wait to get it over with."

Mr. Clack snapped his fingers. "I'll take it! Lead the way."

Frankie slumped towards the school. She should have ditched the exam like she was planning to when Mr. Clack told her about it; face all gentle like he was offering her this amazing opportunity, instead of demonstrating how to swim when she was already under the water with her vision fading out. But she'd woken up early, clammy and tangled in her sheets, and going for a walk seemed like a good alternative to a cigarette. She'd ended up at the school. And then—well, she was already here.

She had to ask for a pencil. Mr. Clark gave her one and

then sat up front with one of the endless science fiction books he read in his classroom at lunch.

Frankie stared down at the exam. Multiple choice. Some questions open-ended. Closed book. Forty-five minutes. Then she'd find out if she had to drag herself out of bed at eight a.m. every weekday for the next couple months.

Mr. Clack looked up. "You can start anytime you want."

Frankie considered getting up and walking out. Slapping the paper on his desk. *Thanks for trying.* But the first question looked...manageable. And the second question, she and Ivy had talked about that in one of their first study sessions. *These violent ends have violent loves...* No, that wasn't right. But Frankie knew if she thought about it long enough, she'd remember.

She sucked in a breath and started scribbling.

Forty-three and a half minutes later, Frankie dropped the test on Mr. Clack's desk.

His head shot up, startled back to reality. He'd been in the middle of an interesting fight scene. "Oh! Are you finished?"

Frankie nodded.

Mr. Clack checked his watch. "We were early. If you want, I can mark it before Homeroom."

Frankie paused, halfway to the door.

"Just to kill the suspense," Mr. Clack said. "We'd like you to be able to pay attention in class today instead of worrying over this."

Sitting there while Mr. Clack decided how the next two months of her life would look sounded like the worst thing in the world. But she could hear students in the halls—nothing loud, just a few who showed up for the free breakfast program

—and the idea of having to see her classmates felt worse. She turned around and headed back to her seat.

"I'll just be a minute," Mr. Clack assured her. "Here, you can have this."

He tossed her his book. It bounced off her desk and spiraled to the floor.

"Durable," he said, and bent over her paper.

Frankie picked up the book. It was about a man who lost his wife in a transporter incident. He tweaked the transporter into a replicator, but the woman who stepped out was not his wife. Or, she was—but there was something else in her, too. Something dark.

Each page intensified her dread. She was almost at the part where the wife reemerged when Mr. Clack slapped the paper down on her desk.

Frankie jumped. "Jesus!"

He grinned. "Had to do it back to you. You passed."

Frankie paused in the middle of tilting her chair back into place. She'd almost rocked it over.

"What?"

"You passed," he repeated. "Want me to go over it again and check?"

Frankie shook her head. On the exam paper sat a bright red *B*. She lifted her hand to touch it. *I have to tell Ivy*. Her hand froze.

"Francesca? You alright?"

In Bulldeen, goodness was something to be looked down on, sneered at, hidden. But here was Mr. Clack, who never raised his voice and never gave up on anyone. If they had another minute, Frankie might have told him everything.

The door opened. Principal Skinner wandered in, rubbing his lined forehead, holding a cigarette. The cheap, familiar kind. Frankie's mouth watered.

"Shit. I mean, shoot." He shoved the cigarette in his jacket pocket. "You're early."

Mr. Clack frowned. "I always show up around now."

"I thought you'd be—Janine said—" Principal Skinner adjusted his glasses. "You should head to the gym. There's going to be an announcement."

"About Frankie's great test results? She just passed her make-up exam."

"What? No." Mr. Skinner gave him a tired, confused look. He was a confused and tired person, but especially so when it came to Mr. Clack. He started to say it, then faltered. He hadn't yet decided how he was going to phrase it.

"There's been an incident."

Frankie stopped counting her yawns as the last students filed into the hall, raising their eyebrows at each other. A surprise assembly never meant anything good, but it was better than Homeroom.

Principal Skinner stood near the door. *Quick exit,* Frankie thought, trying to push down the dread. Everything was fine. She didn't have to do summer school, she *definitely* wouldn't be held back, and whatever this incident was, it had nothing to do with her.

Unless—

Frankie scanned the audience. Her heart hammered, pounding louder in her chest until she saw that familiar straightened head of hair, those glossy lips. Ivy looked distracted, but not horrified, not weighed down with something terrible. She couldn't have gone through with the ritual. Even if she had, they wouldn't have an *assembly* about it. Bulldeen's darkness was only talked about in whispers. Hushed conversations in hallways, schoolyard gossip, shut-down conversations as a parent tucked their child into bed.

Principal Skinner adjusted his shirt collar. It was wrinkled. His parents had never owned an iron, and he carried on the tradition.

"Thank you all for coming," he said, as if any of them had a choice. He looked down. Checking his watch? No, he'd written something on his hand. Jesus.

"It is with great sadness I must tell you that Babe—uh, Henry Simmons died yesterday."

A hush fell over the gym. Heads turned, searching. Frankie searched with them, but none of the dead freaks—Dude, Anna or Jules—were anywhere to be seen.

"It is always a tragedy to lose someone this young," Principal Skinner continued. "His funeral is on Sunday afternoon. We'll let you know more details as they are confirmed."

Frankie filed out of the gym with her classmates, the crowd already buzzing with whispers: *how do you think he died? Where's Dude, do you think there was an accident and he's in the hospital? Is this a really drawn-out play against drunk driving like they did two years ago?* One thing you could count on in Bulldeen: gossip started early.

A prickle at the back of Frankie's neck. She looked around. Ivy was looking back at her from the doorway, face unreadable. The scab near her mouth was growing. Someone walked in front of Frankie, cutting off her view. By the time they moved, Ivy had vanished into the halls.

The school was still thrumming with the news when the last bell rang. Students died, sure, but not often. And not a few weeks before graduation.

So close to getting out, Frankie thought, and then realized she didn't know if Babe was leaving town after graduation. Why wouldn't he? Most people stuck around, but those people had no ambition, options, or desperation. Babe seemed like the kind of guy to have all three. Especially if those whispers about him and Dude were right.

Frankie was still thinking of their elbows brushing while they walked when she turned the corner and a short, solid body slammed into her.

Frankie's back hit the yellow grass, breath knocking out of her. Her head spun.

"Sorry," said a thick voice. "I'm—shit. Sorry."

A hand reached out. Blind with sun, Frankie took it.

Dude Marsh pulled her up. Strong arms. Weirdly skinny legs. Sweat dripped down his forehead. He was sweating hard into his sandals and jeans.

Frankie gestured at his clothes. "Are you running from something?"

Dude stared at her. His eyes were endless. Frankie couldn't help remembering her dreams, waking up sobbing, sure she'd lost something irreplaceable.

"No," he said. "Just...running. I don't know what else—"

His jaw clicked shut. Dude was not a man of many words, but today even this seemed like a struggle.

"Okay." Frankie rubbed her arm, which had taken the brunt of the impact. She didn't want to look him in the eyes again, afraid of the horrible depths. "I'm sorry about...you know. They told us. At school."

Dude's chest heaved. He'd been running for a while. She'd never seen him run before. Dude was a weights guy, not cardio.

There was nothing else to say. Frankie nodded. Dude nodded back. He ran on, and Frankie turned to watch his plodding feet picking up speed, getting faster and faster until he careened around the corner with a desperation she never wanted to feel.

The house was empty. Frankie stood in the living room twisting her rings until her fingers hurt. Then she called Ivy.

"Hel—"

"I passed the make-up test. Your parents come back on Monday. Still on for Sunday night?"

Silence. Static. No, not static—laughter.

"What?"

"Nothing, I was just—I was going to call." Ivy laughed again, disbelieving. "I had my hand on the phone."

Frankie pressed the receiver against her cheek. *Are you sure, are you absolutely sure—*

"See you Sunday," she said, and hung up.

chapter
eight

A STRAY PLASTIC cup from the party sat in the corner of Ivy's hallway, surrounded by an old, stinking puddle of what Frankie hoped wasn't vomit.

"I'm getting to it," Ivy said, as she led Frankie down the hall. "Just—you know, busy."

Frankie nodded, touching a dent in the wall that had definitely not been there last week. "Could pass it off as side effects of bringing Granddad back."

Ivy tossed a look over her shoulder, unsure if she was joking. Frankie wasn't sure either.

"Things got a little wild," Ivy said softly, "after you left. That's what they told me, anyway. I kind of...ran off."

After I kissed you, Frankie filled in.

The scab next to Ivy's mouth was angry red, even under the foundation. Fresh blood beaded underneath. Didn't foundation make open wounds worse? She never put foundation on her popped zits.

"Doesn't that make it heal slower?" Frankie pointed at her own face, mirroring Ivy's.

"What am I supposed to do?" Ivy smiled tightly as she unlocked the basement door. "Let it show?"

"I mean, if you want it to heal. *Yeah*."

They descended the narrow steps. The stairs were engulfed in darkness.

Ivy swallowed. "I left the light on when I was down here earlier."

"Okay," Frankie said, and had to cough to make her voice go back to its normal pitch. "Cool. Whatever."

Frankie set up the candles in a circle on the floor. She'd tried to find long, gothic ones, but the Shop N' Save only had tealights, so tealights it was. It was less creepy ritual and more… fairy ring. Frankie had never seen a fairy ring in real life, but April had this picture book they used to read together. *Step in the middle and be whisked away,* April would whisper, her hair tickling Frankie's cheek, making her giggle.

Frankie held her breath as Ivy stepped into the ring of candles.

Nothing. Ivy turned to look at her expectantly. "What?"

"Nothing." Frankie bent down with her lighter. Ivy's gaze burned a hole in her sharp cheekbone as she crawled from candle to candle, cupping her hand to light each one. There was no wind down here, but she always cupped a hand to light her cigarette. Old habits.

The candles burned. Frankie pocketed her lighter and stood. "Does this mean he's gonna wake up in his grave?"

"I guess." Ivy didn't look bothered by this. She patted her hair down, but it was a lost cause. It frizzed untidily around her ears in a strange pale blotch. Wild hair, almost no makeup, the sore next to her mouth—it made her look otherworldly, almost fae: a strange, savage creature from a fairy tale.

When Frankie couldn't stop herself from looking, she'd caught Marvin glaring at his girlfriend's badly covered scab. At one point he'd picked at the ends of her hair. Frankie had turned away before she could see Ivy's reaction.

Ivy held her hand out. "Can I have the knife?"

Frankie handed over her pocketknife.

"Nixing spell?"

Frankie handed the paper over.

Ivy took it and frowned. "What?" she repeated.

Frankie was still staring. This girl was unrecognizable from the cheerleader from two weeks ago. Frankie knew what her lips tasted like. What she looked like when she was crying, laughing, scrubbing blood from under her nails.

"Nothing," Frankie repeated hoarsely. Babe Simmons' funeral was this morning. Neither of them had gone. "I just... why *Babylove*? Doesn't seem like a name your granddad would come up with."

"Granddad let me name him."

Frankie groaned. Pressed her palms into her eyes until she saw stars. "Okay. Great. Awesome. Do you ever consider he wasn't very good to you? That he wanted to keep you stuck here even when you didn't want to stay, that he was using you, that he didn't care about what you wanted?"

Ivy's fingers curled uselessly around the knife.

"He let me name the cat," she whispered.

"Who cares? This is ridiculous!" Frankie gestured at the candles, the dim basement, the broken cat cage they'd hidden in the corner behind boxes of old clothes, the smashed window covered in duct tape. "What if the nixing spell doesn't work? What if something awful happens?"

Ivy shook her head. "I'm his person."

"Not anymore! He's dead! Let him be dead!"

Ivy opened her mouth. Hesitated. "I promised."

"You were a *kid*."

It was too late. Ivy's eyes were closed, trying to block her out.

"Hey!" Frankie waved her arms. "Don't ignore the safety girl!"

Ivy shushed her. Her hands clenched and unclenched around the knife and paper. Blood at the corners of her nails, constant gnawing.

"Bulldeen I invoke thee," she whispered. "Come and feed."

Silence.

The silence was overwhelming.

Frankie found herself once more holding her breath.

Ivy cleared her throat. "Bulldeen I invoke thee," she said, stronger. "Come and feed."

The candles flickered.

Frankie looked to the window, but the duct tape was holding fast.

She wiped sweat from the back of her neck. A horrifying deja vu crept up her spine rung by rung, like she knew what was about to happen and was powerless to stop it. Was this what she'd been dreaming about? Was this scene, right here, what made her wake up in sweat and screams?

She unstuck her tongue. "Hey…"

Ivy ignored her. "Bulldeen, I invoke thee. Come and feed!"

The candles flickered harder. Wind on Frankie's back, ruffling Ivy's pale hair. A strand caught on her mouth, no gloss, just spit. She didn't bother picking it away as she repeated the incantation, voice growing stronger.

"Ivy," Frankie said. "I think—"

The back of her neck prickled. She turned.

A man stood at the base of the steps, blocking the way out. For a second it looked like a strange amalgamation of Frankie's parents—her dad's dull eyes, her mom's lethal cheekbones— then it was a middle-aged man, tall and sharp in loafers and a long coat. He looked familiar.

Frankie shook. The man said nothing, just smiled. It would

have been a kind smile, if not for his eyes—dark, deep, full of horrible secrets Frankie never wanted to find out.

Frankie whirled back to Ivy, who still had her eyes closed. "Hey—hey! We need—"

Ivy held the pocketknife over her palm. "—invoke thee, come and feed—"

"Nixing spell! Ivy, do the nixing spell!"

Ivy's eyelids shuddered open. For a horrified second Frankie thought they were black, then Ivy blinked and they were blue, her pupils retracting again. Ivy stiffened, her body rigid, her mouth falling open.

"G-granddad?"

"What?" Frankie looked at the thing, which was still a middle-aged man in a long coat. Ivy had shown her pictures of Granddad Wexler in his youth. He looked nothing like that.

"It...for a second, it looked..." Paper crinkled in her hand. Ivy cleared her throat, avoiding its dark gaze.

"Starve the hunger," she said, barely audible over the wind. "Protect us from the one who would consume."

Frankie looked over her shoulder at the man—not man, *thing*, the sharp thing full of terrible secrets. It inclined its head, faintly amused. *Go on.*

A muscle fluttered in Ivy's cheek, slick with sweat. She looked at Frankie desperately.

"I think we should stop," Frankie croaked. Another glance. The thing picked lazily at its razor teeth. "Yeah, let's stop."

Ivy shook her head, dazed. "I can't stop now."

"What? I'm safety girl! You can't ignore safety girl!"

"I—I promised. I'm sorry." Ivy's lip wobbled. Her eyes closed once more. "Bulldeen I invoke thee—"

The blade pressed against her palm, but not *in*, not yet.

Frankie ran into the candle circle. Cold fear as her foot crossed the threshold—but nothing happened, wind still strong, Ivy's voice stronger, the thing looming behind them with a growing smile.

What would you like? The voice echoed in Frankie's head, a faint whisper, but Ivy gasped like it had been a yell.

Spillover, Frankie thought, and grabbed the knife out of Ivy's hand.

Ivy's eyes flew open.

The thing opened its mouth. Even over the wind, its voice was clear. *"What would you like? Give me the blood and it's yours."*

"We want you to fuck off," Frankie screamed, brandishing the knife at him.

The thing smiled. Its teeth were as sharp as the rest of it. *"I wasn't asking you."*

With her free hand, Frankie squeezed Ivy's wrist. "Look at me. You need to stop. The nixing spell didn't work. Nothing good will come from this. I *know* you feel it."

The wind swelled, pressing them apart. Frankie stumbled back, eyes stinging. An old towel hit her in the face, whipped from the box they'd used to hide the cage.

She sheathed the knife and reached out blindly. Cold, biting air.

"Don't even bother with the blood. Just say it and it's yours." The voice intensified, filling the dark basement with its dreadful tones, candles flaring despite the wind, long chains stretching up the ceiling.

Fingers collided with hers. Bitten nails. Spots of blood.

"Say it—"

"Frankie," Ivy yelled, "I have to, I'm sorry—"

"You don't have to do shit except stop this! Ivy, look at me, I'm right here, you just have to—"

"SAY IT!"

"—stop this!"

Ivy stared at her. Frankie was pretty sure. Her eyes were blurry with tears, the wind howling, drowning out their cries.

Frankie reached for Ivy again. "Please!"

A terrifying moment passed.

Ivy's hands stretched out.

Frankie scrabbled. They fumbled, wind still forcing them apart, Ivy grasping her hand and then sliding off. A metallic clatter, barely decipherable in the impossible storm, as Frankie's skull ring went rolling over the concrete.

Their hands closed around each other's wrists.

"BLOOD CAN COME LATER JUST SAY IT ALL YOU NEED TO DO IS SAY—"

"I got you," Frankie gasped, "okay? I'm here."

Ivy stared at her. Her face opened, a realization taking over. Her lips peeled back over her teeth. The first words were lost in the gale, but as soon as they were said, the wind stuttered.

Ivy's mouth kept moving until the wind died down enough for Frankie to hear.

"—take it back! I take it back, go back to whatever weird hole you crawled out of, Granddad can lie there and *rot!*"

Frankie looked back over her shoulder. The thing glitched, gone and then there again, a grimace carved into its features.

Frankie laughed at it. Later she would remember it in patches, the way a bad memory blurs when you look back on it. But that moment, the glint of victory, Ivy's hands solid against hers—that memory would stay with her the rest of her life.

A roar ripped through the basement. At first Frankie thought it was the wind picking up again, but then the roar became guttural.

A voice itched at the back of their heads. Frustrated. Almost satisfied. *Never mind,* it said. *There is another.*

The wind died. The candles burned out. The girls stumbled into each other, no storm to keep them back. Frankie fell against Ivy, chin banging into her shoulder.

"Jesus, sorry—"

"It's fine," Ivy said woodenly.

The hollow of her voice made Frankie stop. She stepped back.

Ivy wiped at her cheeks, tears streaming over her face from the wind. She hunched her shoulders in disappointment.

"Hey," Frankie said, soothing in a way she couldn't remember sounding in a long time. "It's okay, we—"

"I think you should go."

A wave of cold washed over Frankie. "What?"

"Just for now." Ivy hugged her arms. "I...I need time to think."

Frankie tried to bring back the sense of triumph. They'd avoided something terrible. But all she could feel, standing in front of Ivy in the ruined basement, was hollow.

She could have said something. *I'll call you* or *can I help clean up* or even *I saved you from yourself, dumbass! Is this the thanks I get?* But she was tired, adrenaline burning out like the smoking candles, and Ivy was shaking, and Frankie was pretty sure if she said anything else she would start screaming.

So she said, "Okay," and climbed the stairs in silence.

chapter
nine

KNOCK. *Knock. Knock.*

"That is the saddest knock I've ever heard, which means it has to be you," April called. "What do you want?"

Frankie creaked the door open.

"What?" April repeated, eyes on the book on the pillow in front of her. It was a battered copy of Jane Eyre, the only thing their mother passed down to them.

Seconds passed. April looked up, annoyed. "Are you going to say anything, or—hey, what's wrong?"

Frankie shook her head. "Can I get in bed with you?"

April sat up. Frankie hadn't asked since she was eleven and the middle school bullying was at its worst. She frowned, and for a second Frankie thought she'd be told to get lost.

But April pulled back the sheets silently and Frankie climbed in, pressing her head into the crook of April's neck. Light hair tickled her face. Frankie's roots were growing out. Both were in oversized T-shirts and underpants. Neither of them had any makeup on to soften or sharpen their features. If you squinted, you could almost tell they were sisters.

After a while April's hand came up to rest carefully on

Frankie's head. "You were much more comfy when you were smaller."

Frankie dug the point of her chin into April's chest.

"Shit! Little blade bitch." April dug a nail into a tender part of her scalp. Frankie's eyes watered. She'd believed she was so sharp no one could touch her. *What an idiot.*

April settled against the pillow, picking up her book. The lamp was on, and Frankie gazed up at her big sister in the dim light, trying to conjure that pure, adoring love from when they were kids. It was a love shot through with deep annoyance only a sibling could provoke. But the love she remembered was uncomplicated. Easy. No resentment curdling the edges. A love that had never stood in the school hallway screaming *JUST LOOK AT ME, YOU COWARDLY SHIT! WHY ARE YOU DOING THIS? WHAT DID I DO WRONG?*

She wanted to ask, but she'd been shut down so many times it felt pointless. Later, she promised herself. She'd ask later. One day they'd both be grown up and she'd ask, *about you ignoring me in high school*—and April would laugh, say, *oh my god, you still remember that? I was an idiot. So, the story is...*

An innocent assumption teenagers make: that they have more time.

April's chest rose and fell under Frankie's cheek. It wasn't long before sleep tugged at her.

"You know," Frankie mumbled as sleep rolled closer, "You're really nice when you want to be."

April groaned. "Don't tell anyone."

"It's a good thing, jackass."

April smiled. Frankie couldn't see her, but she could tell from her voice.

"It's the kindness," she said, "that kills you."

Their mom said it to them first. She'd met their dad on the

way home from hospital and found him stuck out in the rain two miles from Bulldeen. She'd offered him a ride into town.

Frankie's eyes dragged shut. The dread was still there, waiting, under all that comfort. *It's fine,* she told the dark pit in her stomach. Still it persisted, even as she consoled: *the ritual didn't happen. April will get less bitchy. Ivy...Ivy just needs time. Whatever happens, right now, you're fine.*

The dread dimmed. It didn't vanish, but it sank so far beneath the rare comfort of her big sister's bed that when sleep rose to claim Frankie, she went without a fight.

Knock-knock-knock.

Warmth under her face. Uncomfortable wetness, which Frankie only realized was drool when she wiped her chin. She sat up. Beside her April slumped against the wall, snoring, book in her lap. Sun streamed through the curtains.

Knock-knock-knock.

Who the hell would be knocking right now, Frankie thought muzzily. She checked the clock. Seven a.m. *Seriously, who—*

Panic flooded her as she realized who, exactly, would be knocking on her door at seven in the morning.

She lurched out of bed, falling over her feet until she got to the window. She tugged the curtains back as far as she dared.

Ivy Wexler stood at the front door.

"Shit," Frankie mumbled. She ran downstairs—ignoring April, who threw a pillow at her on the way out, groaning at her to shut up—stopping only to check her reflection in the hallway mirror. Her sleep shirt went down to her knees, thank god. Had Ivy ever seen her without eyeshadow and lipstick? She'd have to deal.

Knock-knock-knock.

Frankie took several slow, composing breaths. Made herself

slouch. Opened the door and leaned on the doorway. "What, princess?"

She tried to make it patronizing. Tried to *sneer* it like she did the first time Ivy came over to her lunch table. But she'd just woken up, and Ivy looked so stupidly beautiful in the morning light, beautiful and uneven and disturbed. She wore a simple blouse and sweatpants. Her hair was unbrushed. Her feet were bare. The scab next to her mouth had faded to tame pink, no new blood at the corners.

Frankie frowned at Ivy's feet. "Where the hell are your shoes?"

Ivy looked down at them. Her toes flexed against the steps, surprise flitting across her face. She'd run out the door so fast she hadn't realized.

She swallowed. "Babe Simmons is back."

Sleep was too close. Frankie didn't understand. And then she did.

"Has anything...happened?"

Ivy nodded. "That homeless man outside the Shop N' Save —they found his body." She toyed with her hands. Band-Aids adorned the tips of every finger. She'd picked her cuticles clean. "They're saying it's wild dogs, but..."

Frankie nodded, dazed, mind full of razor teeth and tearing flesh. *Wild dogs.* What was that man's name again? Leroy, she thought. Leroy someone.

"I think you made the right call," Ivy whispered. "Stopping it."

Frankie felt herself nod again. A warm breeze skimmed her bare legs. Summer in Bulldeen.

The relief hit her all at once, but it wasn't overwhelming. It stuck in the background, just like the dread: yes, they'd avoided something terrible, but it had still arrived. They just had to hope it stayed adjacent to them, that it would rush past without sucking them up in its orbit.

Ivy held out a hand. On her middle finger, a glint of silver.

"It took a while," Ivy said, sliding the skull ring off. "But I found it."

Frankie looked at it resting in Ivy's palm. Her stomach twisted. "Keep it. It looks good on you."

Ivy blinked rapidly. "Oh! Okay."

It slid back home on her middle finger. Ivy rubbed it, bandaged fingers immediately finding the eyeholes.

Frankie waited. Ivy's mouth kept opening, closing, breath stuttering like she kept meaning to say something but couldn't quite do it. An apology, maybe. Or some terrible news she was holding back.

"Want to walk to school together?"

Another breeze on Frankie's knees. Frankie didn't notice.

"When it's time, obviously." Ivy waved at her lack of pants. "And after you get dressed."

Frankie snorted down at her bare feet. "Look who's talking."

"Right." Ivy frowned again. "Yes."

Babe Simmons is back. Frankie shuddered, thinking of coffins, decay, Dude Marsh—because of course it was Dude Marsh, the only question was whether the girls had joined in. They were always too close, that friend group. It seemed natural to imagine the three of them standing over his grave, holding out their bleeding palms. She and Ivy had never seen what happened after you gave your blood, and she never wanted to find out.

Frankie rubbed her face. Her brain was still half asleep, it was taking longer to catch up.

"What about Marvin?"

"We broke up." Ivy bit her cheek. "I broke up with him."

"Good. He sucked."

Ivy barked a laugh. "He did kind of suck!"

Frankie dried her damp hands on her baggy shirt. "Thought you hated being walked to school."

"I don't think I'll mind if it's you."

Frankie nodded like that wasn't the best thing she'd ever heard, like there wasn't a dead man walking around town eating homeless people.

"Want to come in for breakfast? My parents aren't out yet, so we'll have to eat it in my room, but—"

"Okay." Ivy smiled, small and sweet.

More awful things were coming, but not yet. Right now they had cereal to eat and clothes to borrow. They had this: Monday morning, barefoot and sweating, Frankie holding the door open for Ivy to step inside.

END

Want to find out what happens next for Frankie and Ivy?

Turn the page for a sneak peek...

sugarsnap preview

Keep reading to see a preview of the next installment: SUGARSNAP.

The summer of 2004 was infused with the strange, inexplicable feeling that something terrible was going to happen.

This was partly correct. Something terrible had already happened in Bulldeen, and there was more to come—but not yet. In the cafeteria of Bulldeen High, something else was growing. Something sweet and kind. An Eden in the shape of a plastic table.

Frankie didn't notice Ivy until a small, smooth hand stroked her shoulder.

"Jesus!" Frankie jumped, whirling in time to see Ivy's bemused expression, her red lips creasing into a grin.

Frankie sighed. "Sorry. I didn't hear you come up."

"It's fine." Ivy Wexler sat across from her. They used to sit next to each other, but it had raised too many eyebrows. Her sneaker bumped Frankie's boot under the table. "How was English?"

"Ugh. How was AP?"

"*Ugh*," Ivy said, in a decent impression of Frankie's groan.

Frankie Tanner did her best not to look charmed. She turned her boot against Ivy's sneaker and her clean white socks. Ivy was in her cheerleader uniform again. Up until last year it was a constant sight. Now she only wore it twice a week when she had after-school practice. She was the lone cheerleader who had broken away from her squad's table to sit with Loser Tanner in their little corner.

The cheerleader table was its usual flurry of white and red skirts. Once upon a time, Frankie's sister, April Tanner, sat with them, making fun of the less popular and stealing people's milk.

"Hey." A crimson nail brushed Frankie's wrist. "You okay?"

"Fine," Frankie said immediately. Like she was going to say anything else in this place. "Heard your squad bitching about getting ash on their shoes from practice. That's bull, right?"

"You've been in the gym! I think it still *smells* like smoke, but everything's intact. *Finally.*"

Frankie hummed in agreement. The gym burned down at the end of their freshman year. Now they were at the start of junior year, and the gym had only just been re-opened after over a year of using the field and canceling gym when it rained. Students complained about a charcoal stench and black streaks on their ankles. Frankie didn't smell anything, and her shoes were always clean after gym. But the room still gave her the creeps.

We know it's a lot to deal with, Principal Skinner had said after he pulled her into his office two weeks ago. *Especially for you, after...what happened. But you can't just not go to class.*

Frankie had seriously considered spitting on him. But she wanted to graduate next year. So she'd gritted her teeth and said, *yes sir.* And she'd walked into the gym and run laps on the floorboards April bled out on.

They still hadn't told her how someone could bleed out during a fire.

"Frankie?"

Frankie startled. "What?"

Ivy tugged at her hair. The blonde dye had almost completely grown out, so her hair was light brown except for the ends. "Are you sure you're—?"

A shriek drowned her out. Frankie whirled, heart in her throat.

A cheerleader had her hands over her mouth and was staring teary-eyed down at her footballer boyfriend. In his hands was a sign with the words spelled out in glitter: WILL YOU GO TO HOMECOMING WITH ME?

"Yes," the cheerleader, whose name was Debby, sobbed, as if this was a marriage proposal and not a dance that happened every year. "A thousand times yes!"

She leapt into his arms. Uproarious applause followed from the cheerleaders' table, scattered applause from everywhere else.

The cafeteria soon turned back to its dull chatter. Bulldeen High had been quieter since the gym burned down. It didn't help that the thornfruit fields, Bulldeen's only export and the sole reason the town stayed alive, had died around the same time. People were fleeing in droves as section after section of the thornfruit factory closed down, and businesses went bust. The Homecoming game had been canceled, with too many footballers leaving and no one stepping up to fill their positions.

It wouldn't be long before Bulldeen was a ghost town.

Ivy rolled her eyes at Debby embracing her boyfriend. "She doesn't even *like* him."

"Who would?"

Ivy giggled. "Right? Zit city. Ew." She flipped her hair over her shoulder, and the thought struck Frankie how derisive she would've been about that gesture a year ago. Now all she felt was fondness and longing, both of which she schooled carefully out of her expression as Ivy continued, voice lowering: "Would you do one of those corny proposals, if you could?"

Frankie pressed her lips together to stop her smile from getting out of control. She could feel her black lipstick smudging. She'd have to reapply it before class.

"Why am I proposing?" she whispered. "Where's *my* proposal?"

"Do something to deserve one." Ivy flipped her hair again, taking care to almost hit Frankie in the face, giggling when Frankie scowled. "So? What would you do?"

Their shoes brushed once again under the table. Casual. Almost incidental.

Frankie leaned forward. "I wouldn't do it like that idiot. You don't want something public, in front of everyone."

"I don't?"

"No. You want something private. Secluded. I'd...I don't know, I'd put fairy lights all over your room when you were in the shower and turn all the lights off, and when you came out, I'd be kneeling on the carpet. Or whatever."

Ivy's teasing grin turned soft and knowing. "Would you make me a sign?"

"Yeah, sugarsnap. I'd make you a sign."

They stared at each other under the fluorescent lights. For a moment there were no high schoolers carving circles in tables, no lunch lady calling for more meatloaf, no teachers speaking in hushed tones about another cat found with its throat ripped out. It was just the two of them: Ivy and Frankie, against the world.

Frankie pushed the tip of her boot against Ivy's socks. "Do you wanna—"

"Yes," Ivy said.

As make-out spots went, a high-school toilet stall was not ideal. In their defense, they were 2004-era lesbians in small-town Maine. They couldn't sneak behind the field or find an empty classroom. Any kissing outside of their bedrooms required walls and no windows.

"Just two more years," Ivy said into Frankie's neck. "Then we get the hell out of here. Go to New York."

Frankie nodded. It was hard to think with Ivy's mouth on her neck, Ivy's hands on her waist, Ivy's lavender perfume against her face. She would have agreed to anything. *Flush my head down the toilet? Yes ma'am, whatever you say.*

The door creaked open. Frankie bit down on her lip, silencing her moan.

"—kind of excited to see them die," said Madeline Grisham, who was repeating senior year for the third time. "You know? Like, our parents looove those fields, thornfruit made the town, blah blah. But you can't say there wasn't some satisfaction in watching everything shrivel up and *rot*. Right?"

"Die die die, baby," said Selena Grisham, three years younger than her sister, also in senior year.

The faucets turned on. Water splattered into basins. In their tiny stall, Frankie set her forehead against Ivy's, waiting, Selena's voice on a loop in her head. *Die die die, baby.* It sounded like a song with a name she couldn't remember.

"Kind of disappointing," Madeline continued, the words slurred, as if she was pulling her bottom lip up to check for chin blemishes. "Like, it's just one. But still."

"It's not like rats—can I have that?" Rustling noises of a makeup bag being opened. "Thanks—one might just mean *one*. It's the first that's grown in over a *year*, Mads."

"Yeah, and I was—gimme that, you always use too much—

I was *sooo* happy to see it die! Someone should throw a party. That should be the Homecoming theme: Bulldeen is dying, let's shoot confetti cannons for the funeral."

Ivy's head came up. The fine hair of her brows tickled Frankie's neck as they pulled inwards. Frankie held her breath.

The taps stopped. Lips smacked. The sisters had traded lip gloss.

"I hate this goddamn place," said Madeline coldly. "I hope that plant shits itself before the week is up. I hope somebody burns those plants and salts the earth. Free us from this shithole."

Free us, Frankie mouthed against Ivy's cheek. She'd never agreed with Madeline on anything before today.

"Anyway," Madeline sighed. "They found another cat. Throat ripped out. Who do you think—"

"I mean, they're saying it's dogs?"

"It's not *dogs,* ugh. You're such a wasteoid..."

Footsteps. The sisters' chatter died as the bathroom door swung shut.

Frankie let out her breath. Stepped back. "The bell's gonna go. We should—"

Ivy stared at her, face pale.

Frankie's heart thumped. "What?"

Ivy just looked at her.

"It's fine," Frankie said. "It's—it's just one plant. Bulldeen's practically signed its death certificate. This doesn't mean anything. The cats, neither."

Ivy's hand fluttered up to scratch next to her mouth.

"Don't." Frankie caught it. It was Ivy's worry spot, and it had finally started bleeding last year during all the resurrection crap that brought the girls together. It had scabbed for weeks before finally healing over.

Ivy's fingers curled in hers. She squeezed, then went over to the sinks. She wet a paper towel and dabbed Frankie's black lipstick from her face and neck. Frankie busied herself reapplying said lipstick, a thick dark layer to match her hair.

Their eyes met in the mirror.

"It's fine," Frankie said. "We don't even know—it might not have anything to do with all of Bulldeen's...magic shit."

Ivy looked less than convinced. Frankie couldn't blame her. Ivy's granddad's resurrection had been averted right before anything got locked in, but for months after the ritual they had nightmares about the creature. That strange, shapeshifting figure in the corner of the basement, sloughing into the people who had hurt them the most—but never all the way. The face was always too sharp, teeth too long, body too tall.

Then the real resurrection happened. Babe Simmons, a senior, died just before the school year ended. The day of his funeral, he was up and walking around again. The murders started not long after that.

Ivy and Frankie stayed the hell out of it. They stayed away from Babe and his friends, dubbed "The Dead Freaks." They didn't participate in the Zombabe gossip, which only got louder the more bloodshed ramped up. Then everything came to a crescendo: notorious bully Hunter Creel attacked one of the Dead Freaks, set his own friend Moe on fire, burned down the school gym and somehow ended up dying inside it. They heard he attacked the police chief, Kate Higgins. They heard he didn't die of smoke inhalation. That he died of *blood loss*, like April Tanner.

They heard the Dead Freaks, plus Chief Higgins, drove away from the fire like something was after them—or they were after something. They heard the thornfruit fields started dying that same day. They heard Babe Simmons' valedictorian speech was ominous and *weird*, and that he and the Dead Freaks got the hell out of Bulldeen right after.

Frankie and Ivy heard a lot of things. They didn't ask.

Frankie cupped her girlfriend's uncertain face.

"Two years," she said. "Then New York."

Ivy nodded, and the trust in her eyes made Frankie's chest throb. The moment was only slightly marred by Frankie's yawn, her jaw cracking.

"Tired baby," Ivy cooed. Frankie swatted at her.

Sincerity crept into Ivy's tone. "Bad dreams?"

Rotting thornfruit fields stretching beyond the horizon. Sharp, familiar cheekbones. Strange songs, the lyrics forgotten upon waking. Guilt rising like smoke, thick enough to choke.

"Nope," Frankie said, popping the P. It was a lie, and they both knew it. But Ivy nodded, the two of them sharing another moment of being *FrankieandIvy* before heading back out into the world—

—and straight into Marvin Martin, mediocre footballer, perpetual polo shirt wearer, and Ivy's ex-boyfriend.

"Jesus," Frankie spat, reeling back. "Watch where you're going, asshole."

Marvin smiled tightly, and Frankie caught up: he'd been *standing* outside the girl's bathroom, not walking by.

Fear and anger rolled through her in equal measure. She prepared an eyeroll and a growl, and failing that, the knife she kept in her back pocket.

"Always found it weird, girls going to the bathroom together," Marvin drawled.

"I always found it weird when boys stand outside girls' bathrooms," Frankie replied flatly. "Scram, Marvin."

Marvin's gelled hair stayed perfectly still as he cocked his head. "You know what? *I* think what's weird is you girls spending *twenty minutes* in there."

Shit. Frankie opened her mouth, but Ivy beat her to it.

"Women's troubles," she said, sweetness ringed with

venom. *There* was the cheerleader Frankie used to loathe, repurposed to defend her girlfriend. "You wouldn't understand. I seem to remember you screaming like a little girl that time you found a tampon in my purse. Did I ever tell you about that, Frankie?"

"No, you did not."

"He *shrieked*, Frankie."

"Did he, Ivy?"

Marvin snarled, "I didn't *shriek*. I was just surprised. You shouldn't keep those things lying around where unsuspecting guys can see them."

He stepped in close to Ivy. Frankie's hand locked around the knife in her pocket. If this little shit tried anything...

"Are you high?" He scanned Ivy's face worriedly. "Did she get you high, Ives?"

Frankie laughed. "Oh my god, leave us *alone*."

"Don't call me Ives," Ivy said, and took Frankie's wrist. "Let's go."

Marvin called her name down the hall. Ivy didn't stop until they were around the corner.

"He's so *annoying*," she barked. "I can't believe him. Am I high? I'm at *school*!"

The bell rang. Students streamed around them.

The girls set off for English. Their hands bumped, incidental. Frankie kept her eyes ahead and told herself Marvin was the biggest thing they had to worry about, Marvin and not being able to go to Homecoming together, Marvin and this homework assignment coming up she hadn't started yet.

Marvin was their worst threat, she assured herself, as they slid into their seats on opposite sides of the room. Nothing else.

Check out Book 2 SUGARSNAP now!

thank you

Thank you so much for reading Babylove! If you want to support me, please leave a review on Goodreads, Amazon and any social media of your choice.

You can get updates on my upcoming LGBT YA books by subscribing to my newsletter! Sign up by visiting my website at isbelleauthor.com.

You can also follow me on Tiktok @i.s.belle_writes.

acknowledgments

A hearty thank you to Edward Giordano for formatting, Catriona Turner for her editing, and Laya (Rose) Mutton-Rogers for the cover art.

And who could forget my lovely beta readers? Y'all are awesome.

about the author

I. S. Belle is a Young Adult author who lives in New Zealand. She works in a bookstore and stops to pat dogs in the street.

She received a Creative Writing Masters from the International Institute of Modern Letters.

also by i. s. belle

BABYLOVE SERIES

BABYLOVE

SUGARSNAP

SWEETHEARTS - Coming January 2024

ZOMBABE SERIES

ZOMBABE

ZOMBABE #2 - Coming Soon

ZOMBABE #3 - Coming Not As Soon